FREE Bonus
SEE LAST PAGE

I0446921

This Book Belongs To:

_____

_____

_____

Merry Christmas

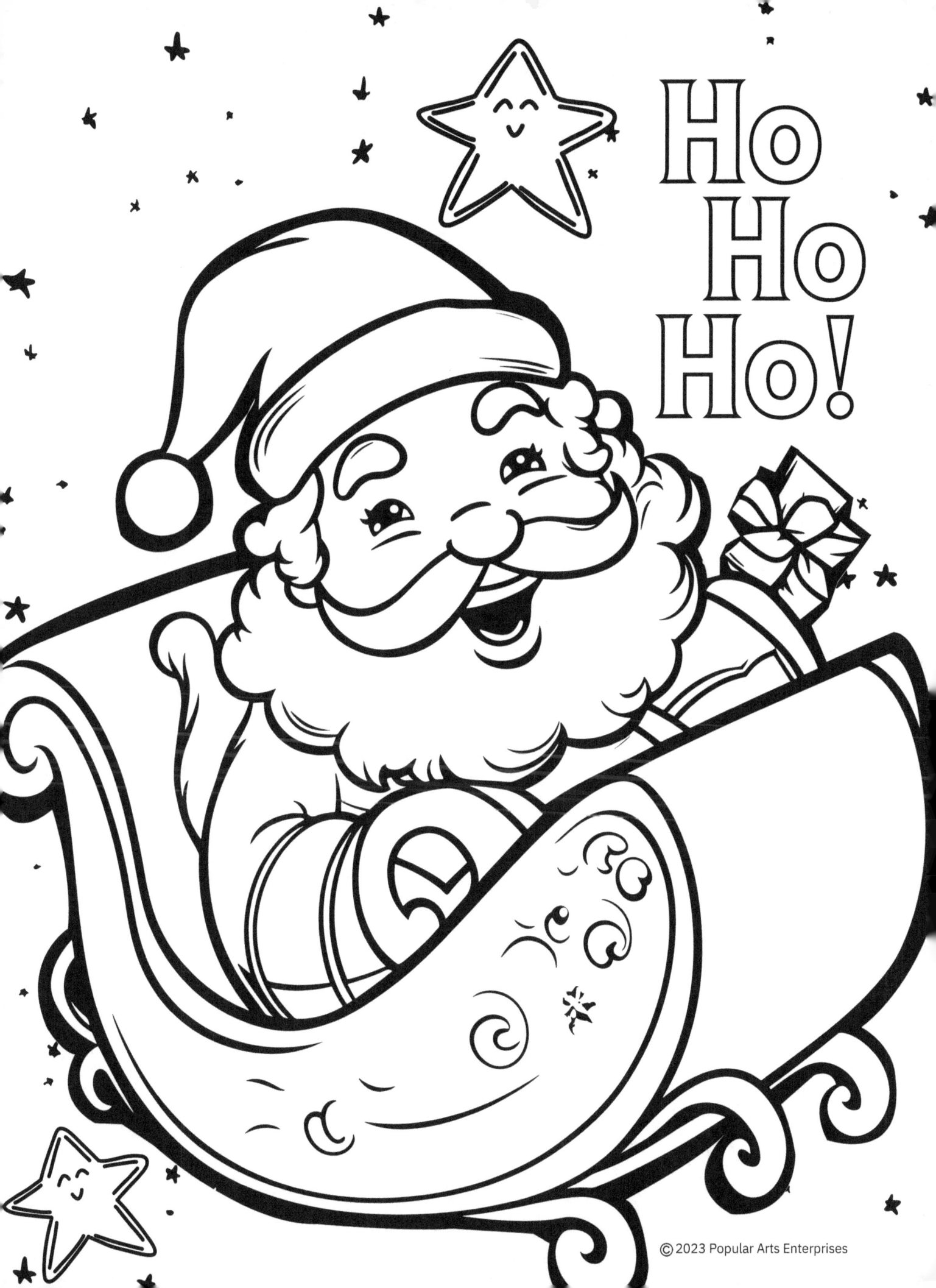

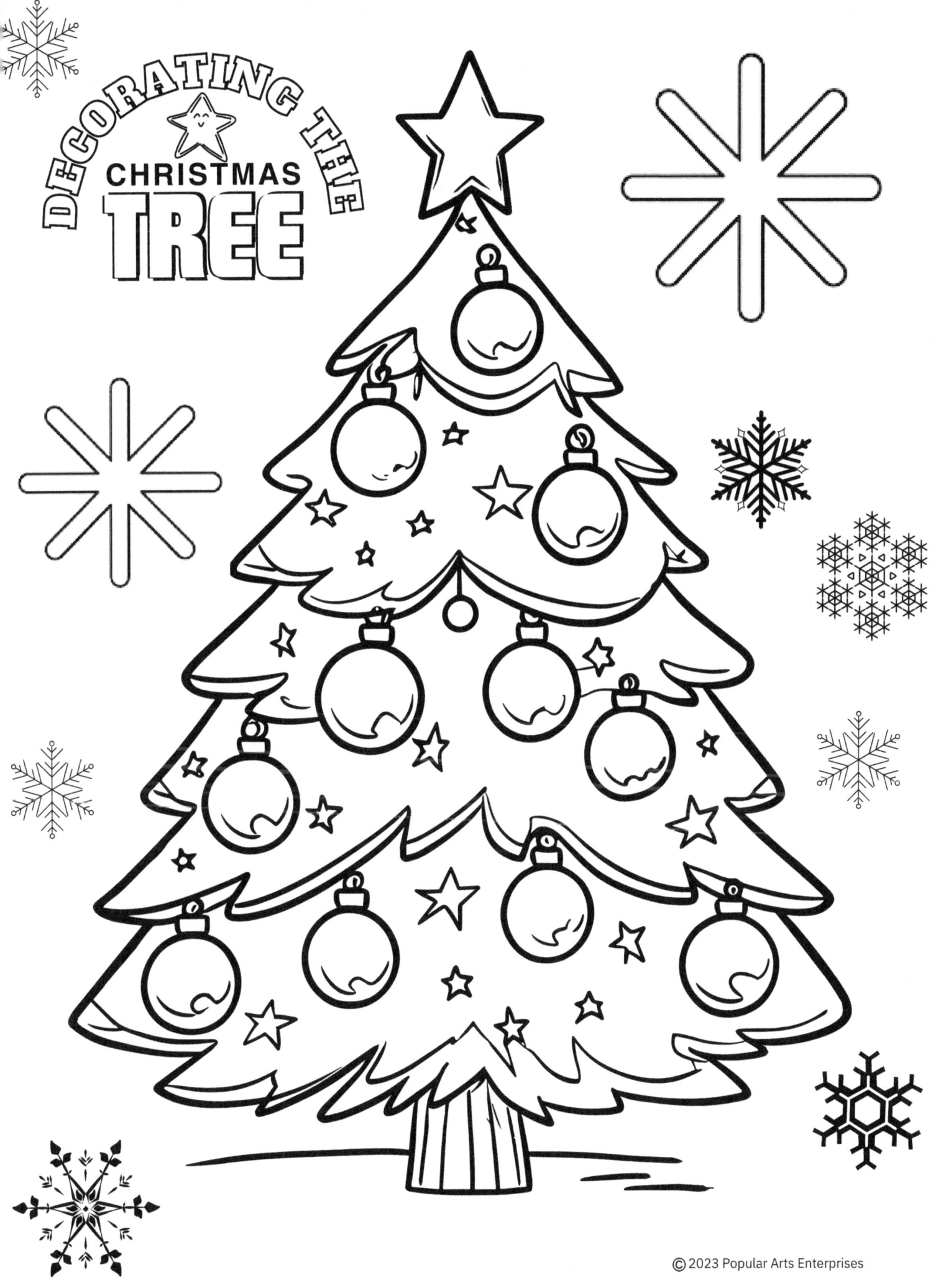

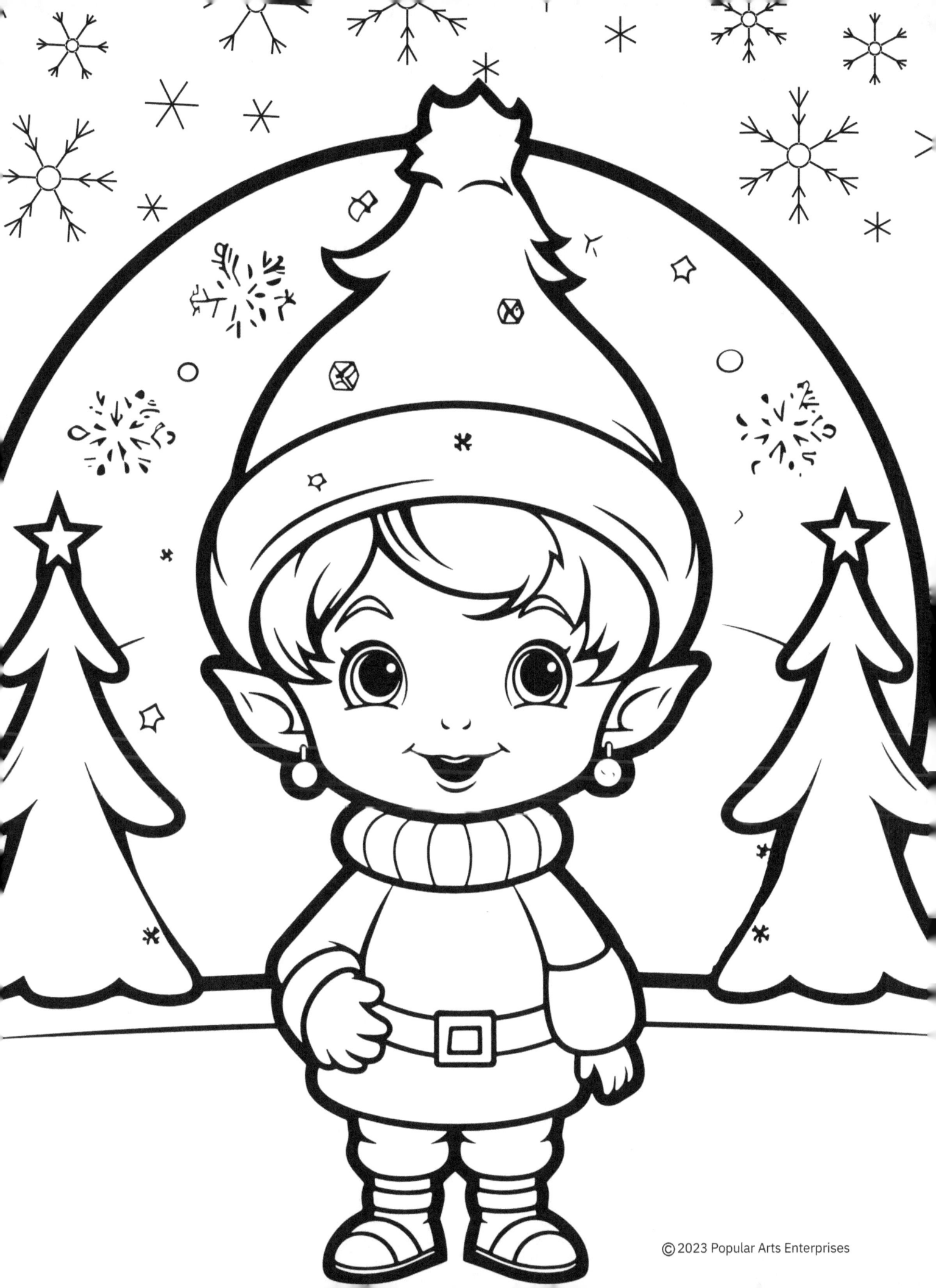

Sweet CANDY

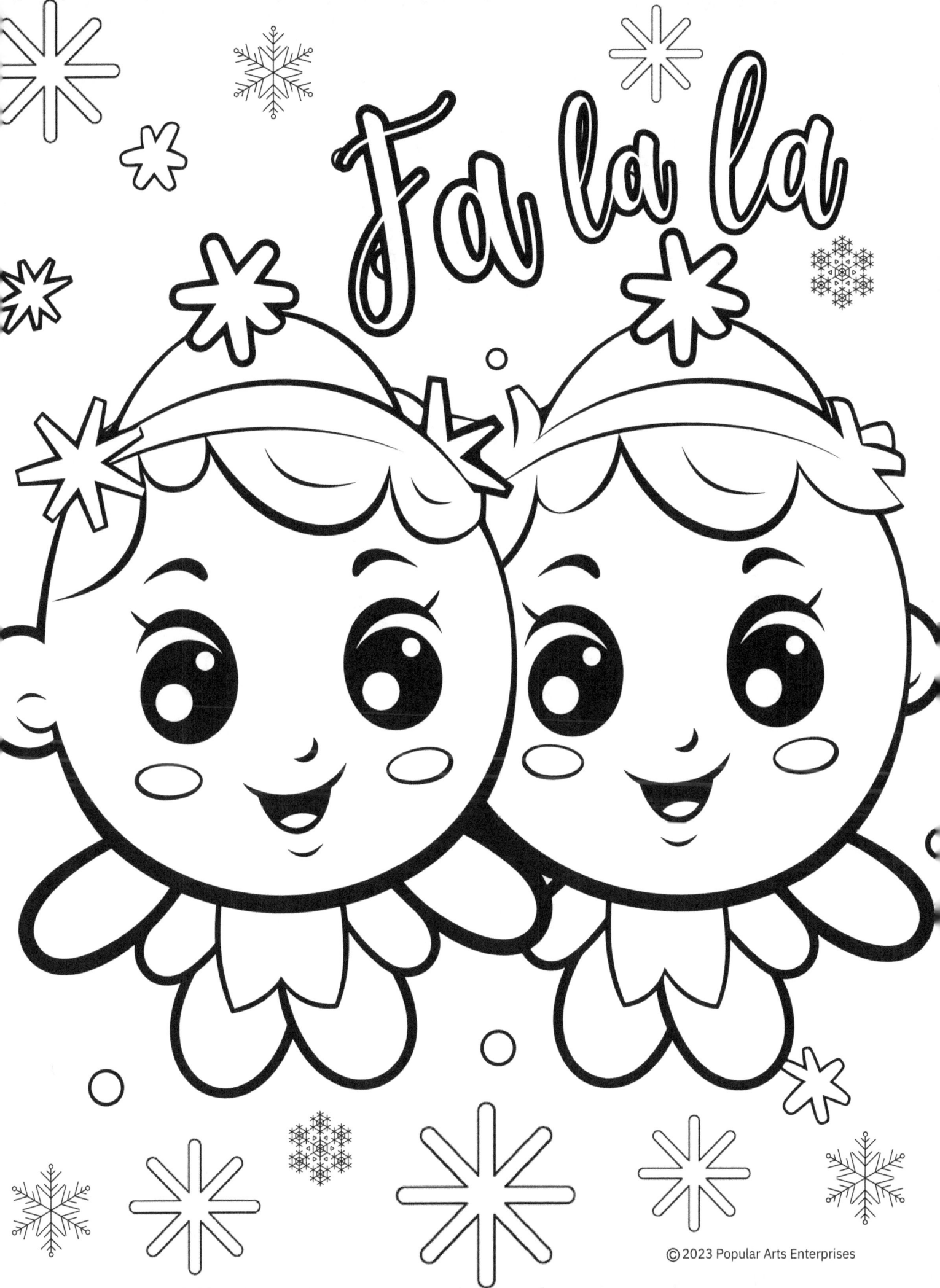

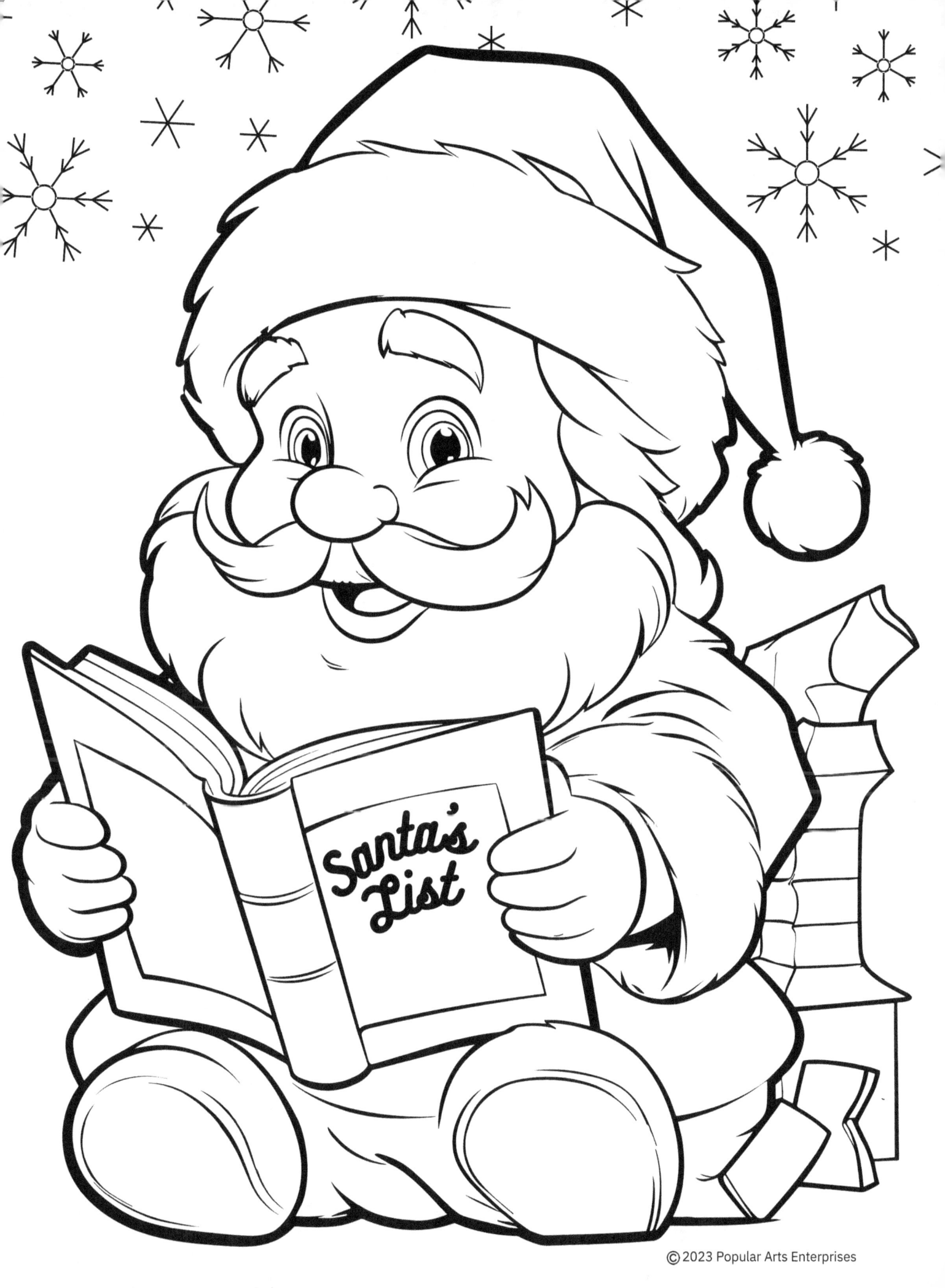

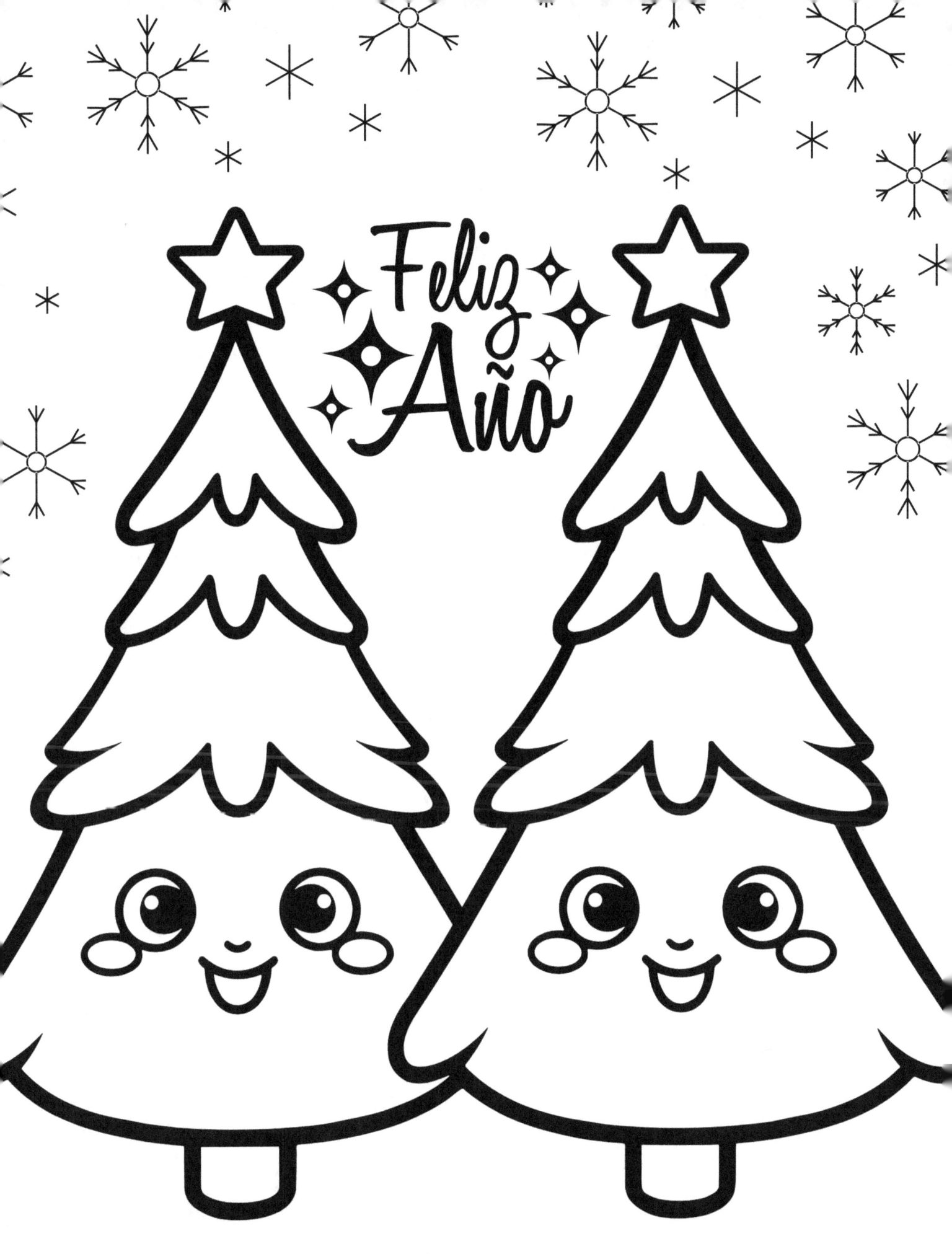

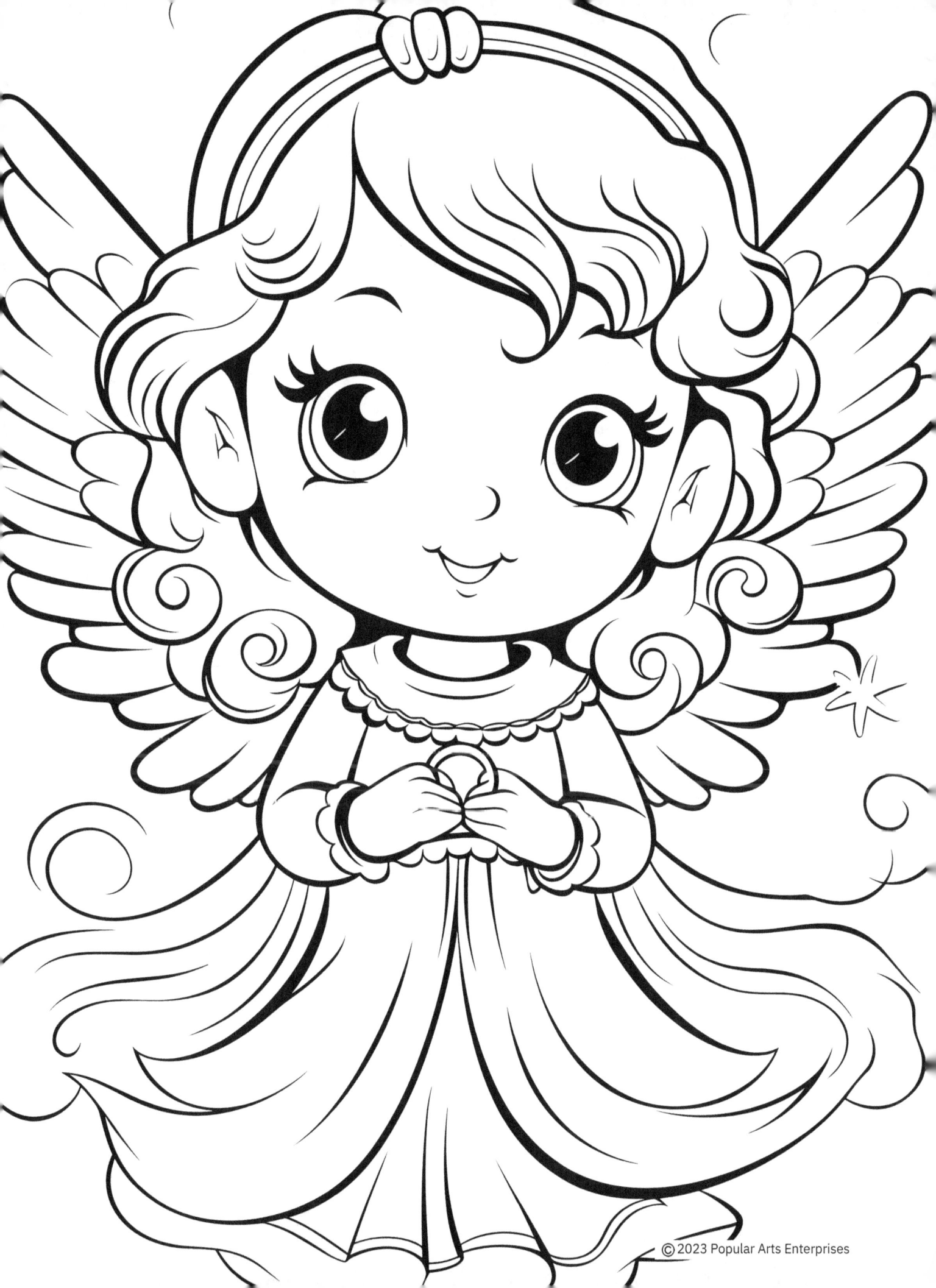

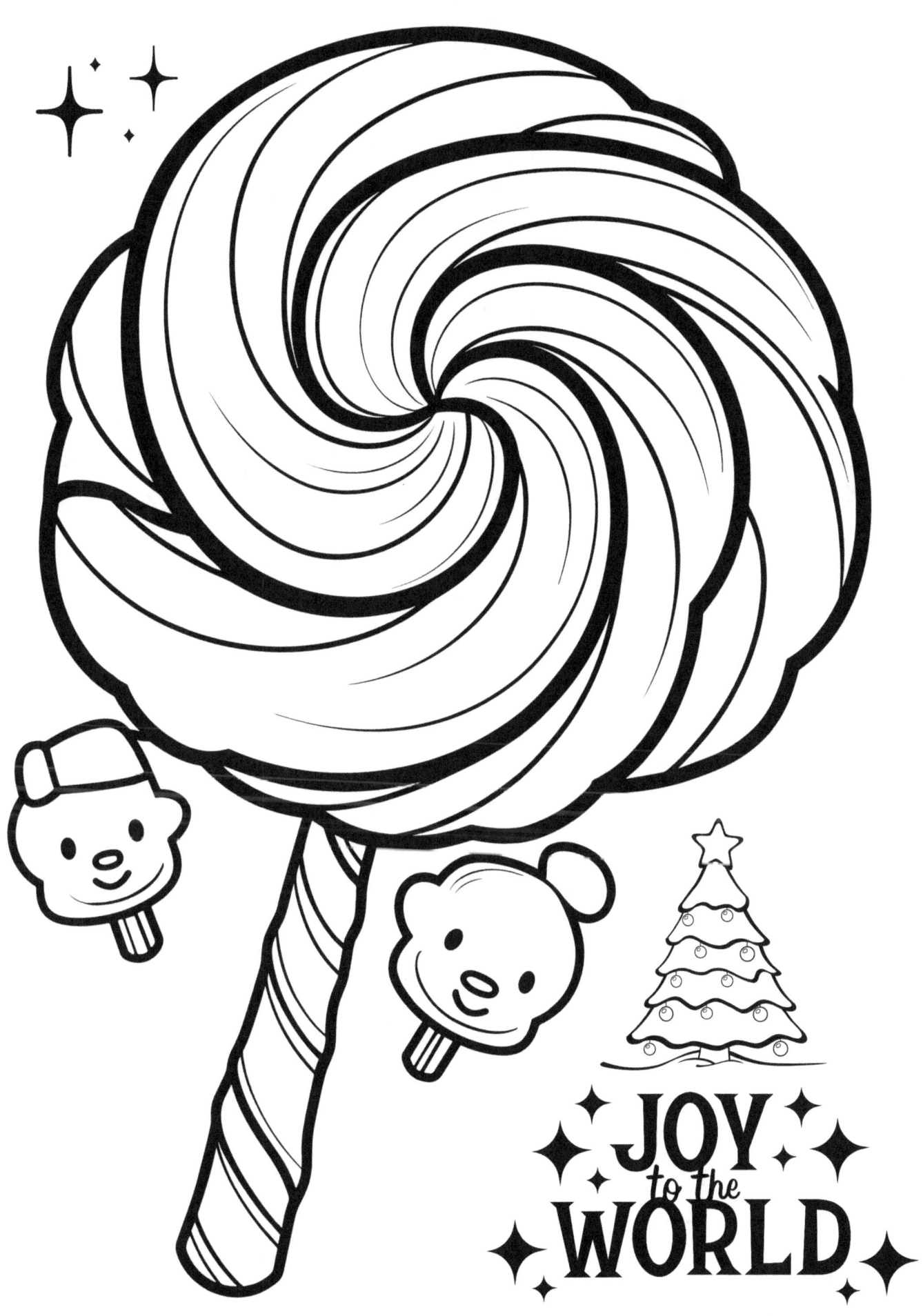

JOY to the WORLD

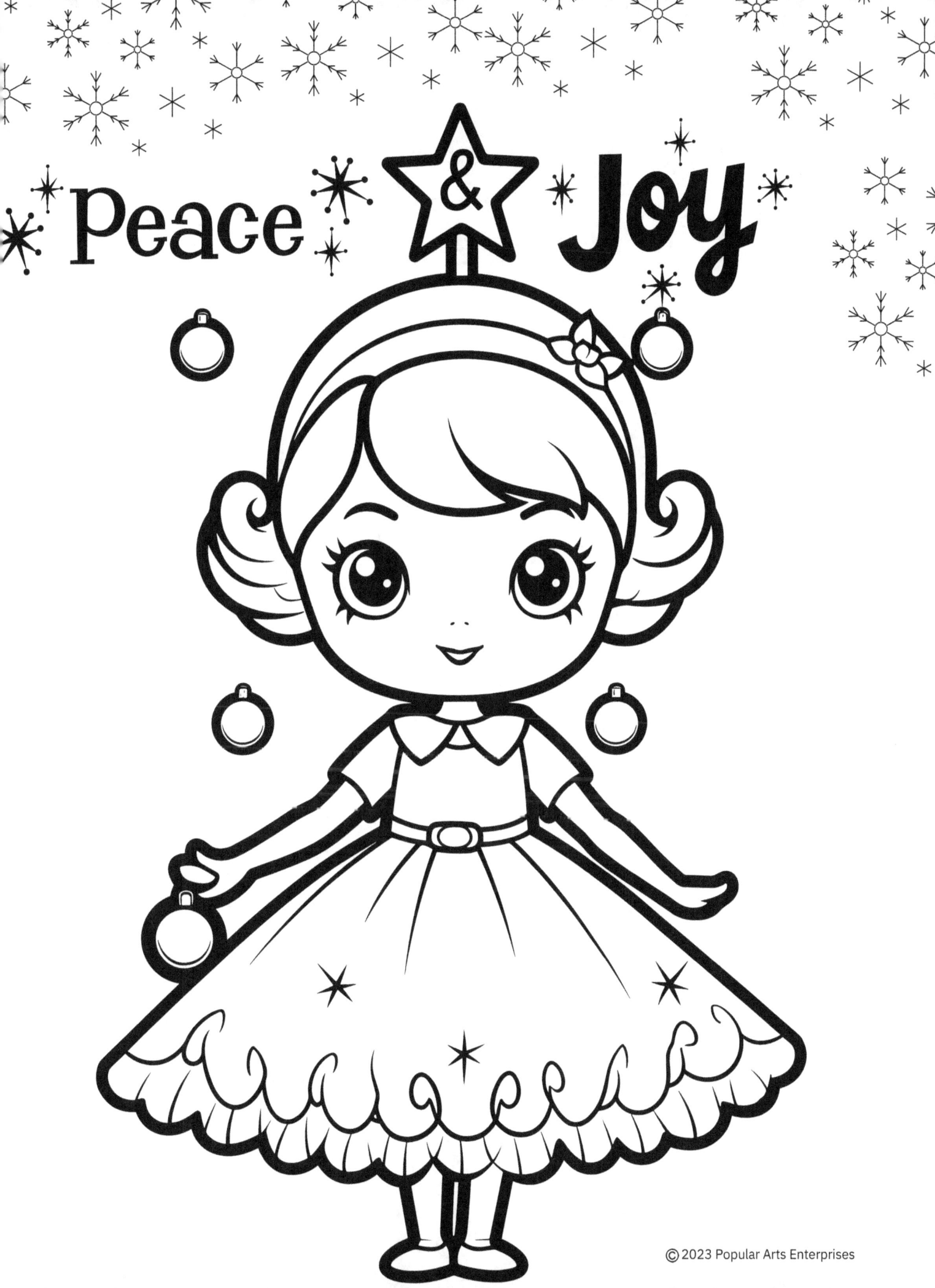

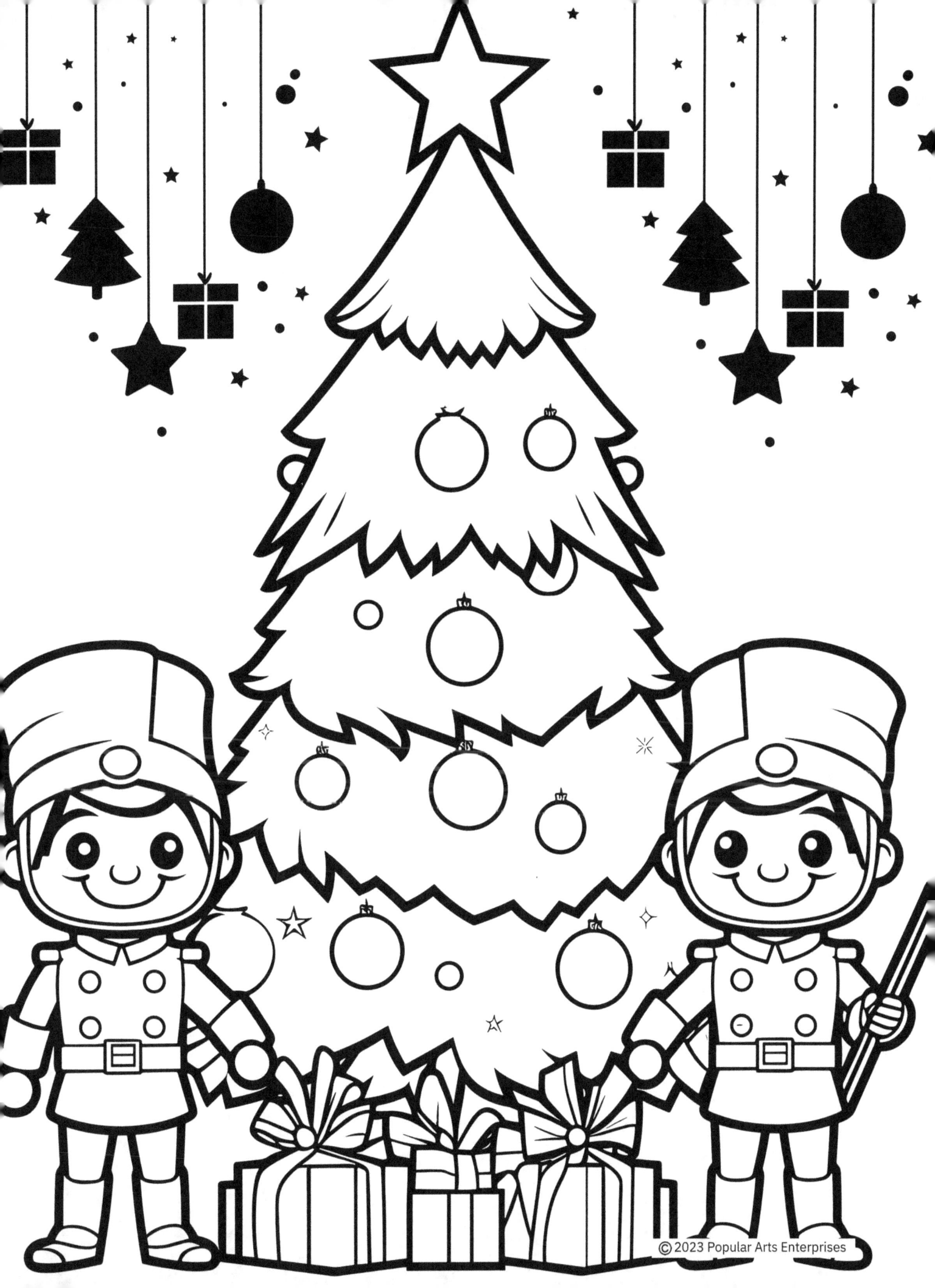

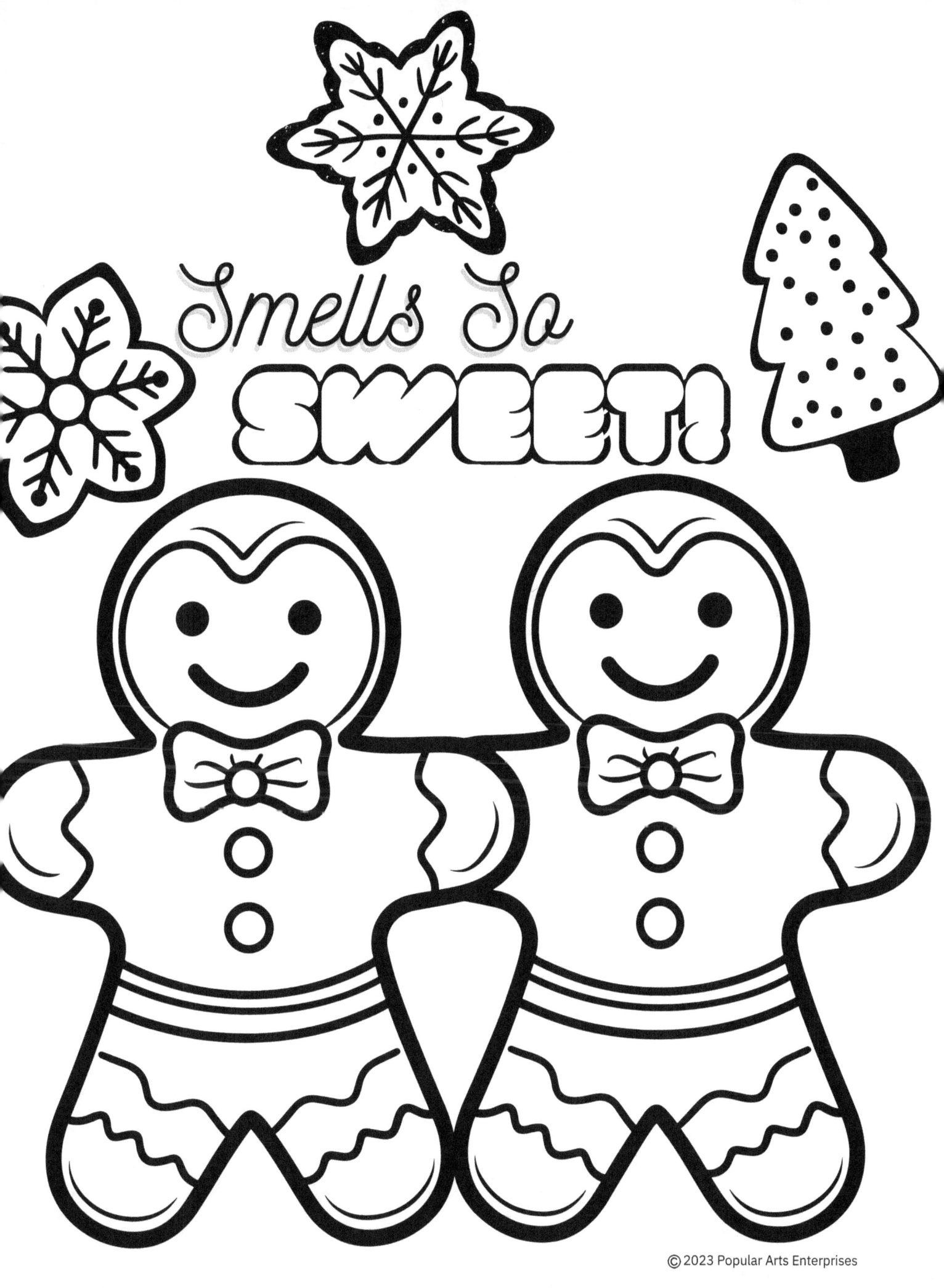

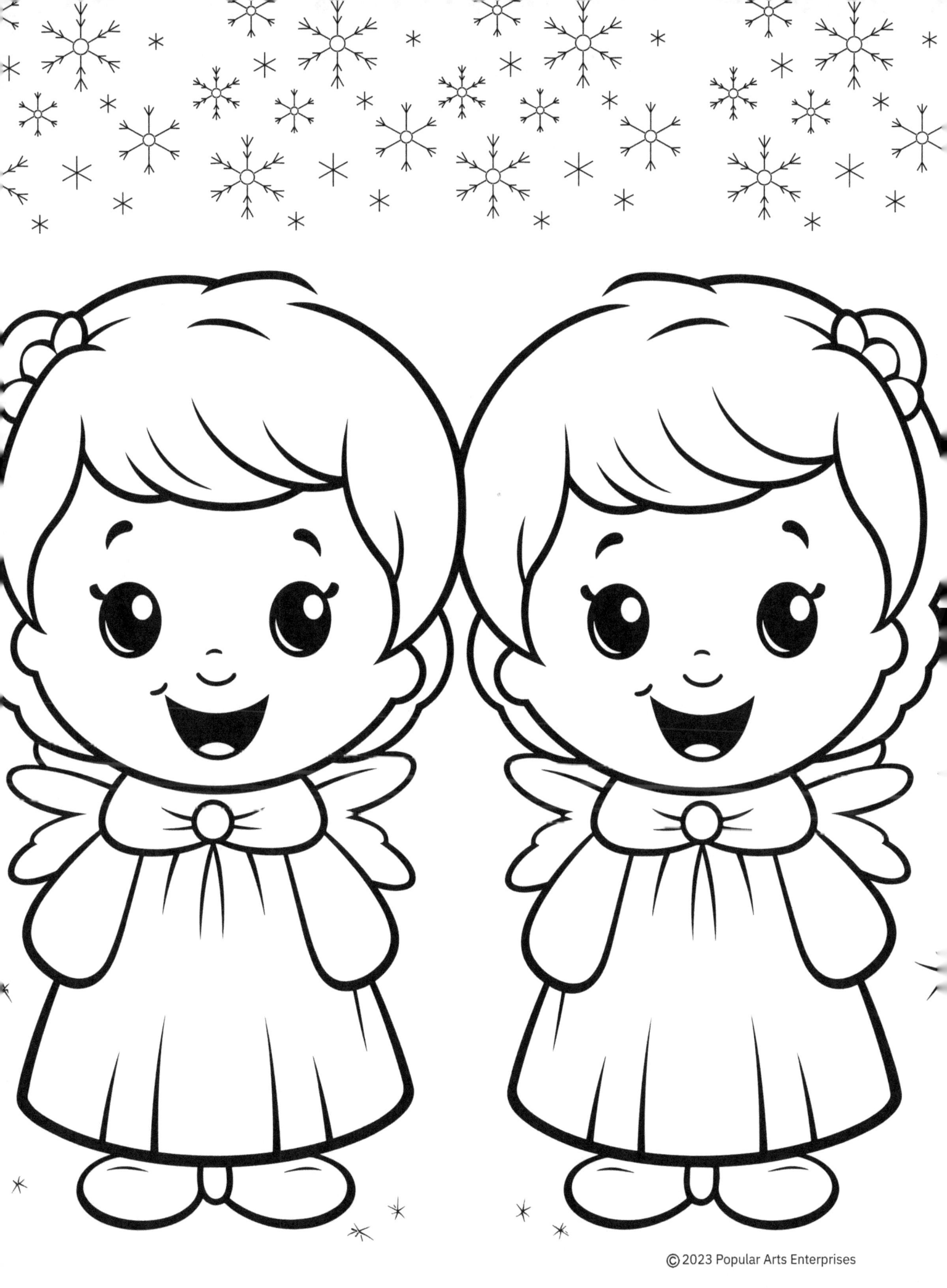

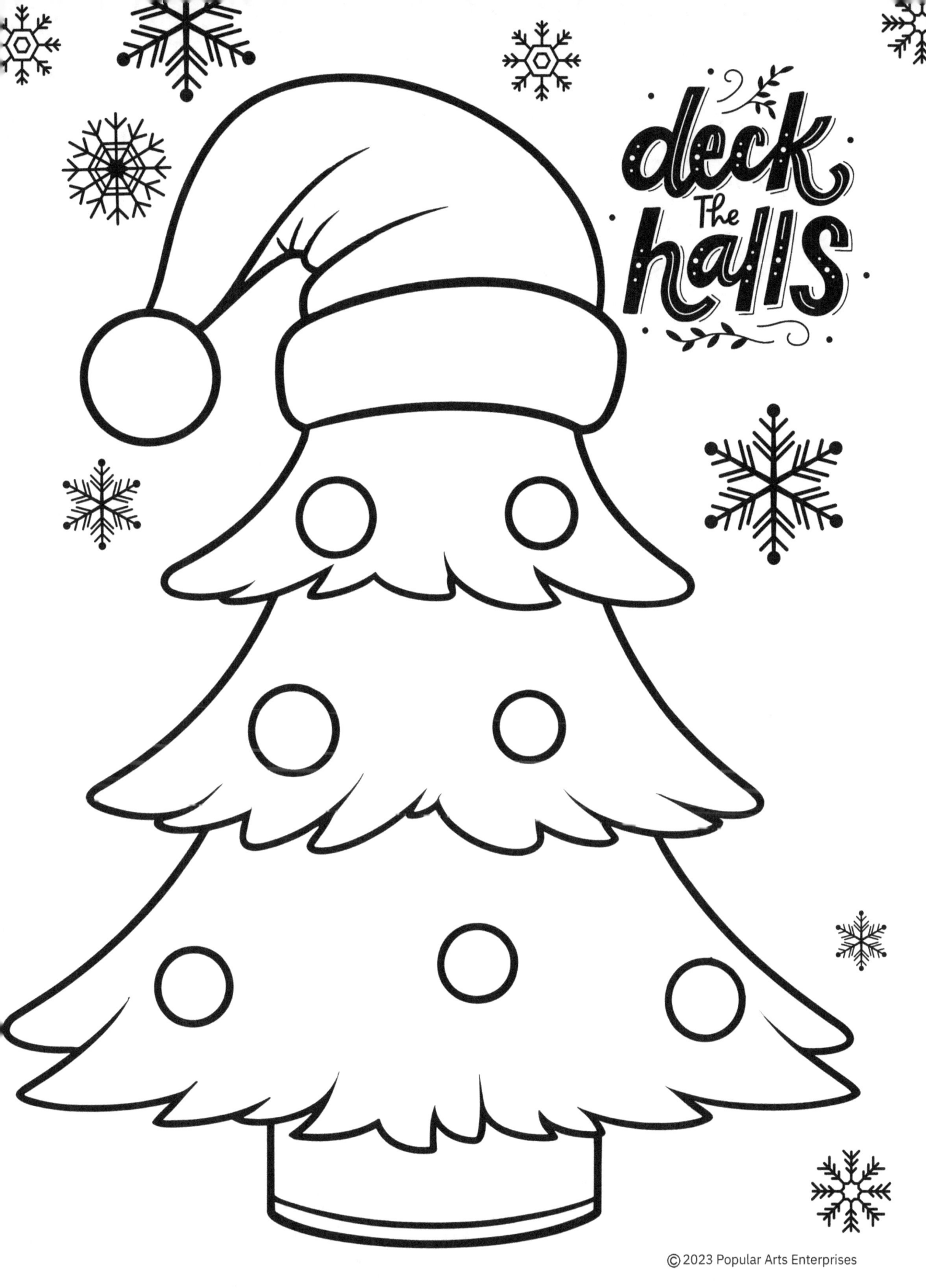

deck
The
halls

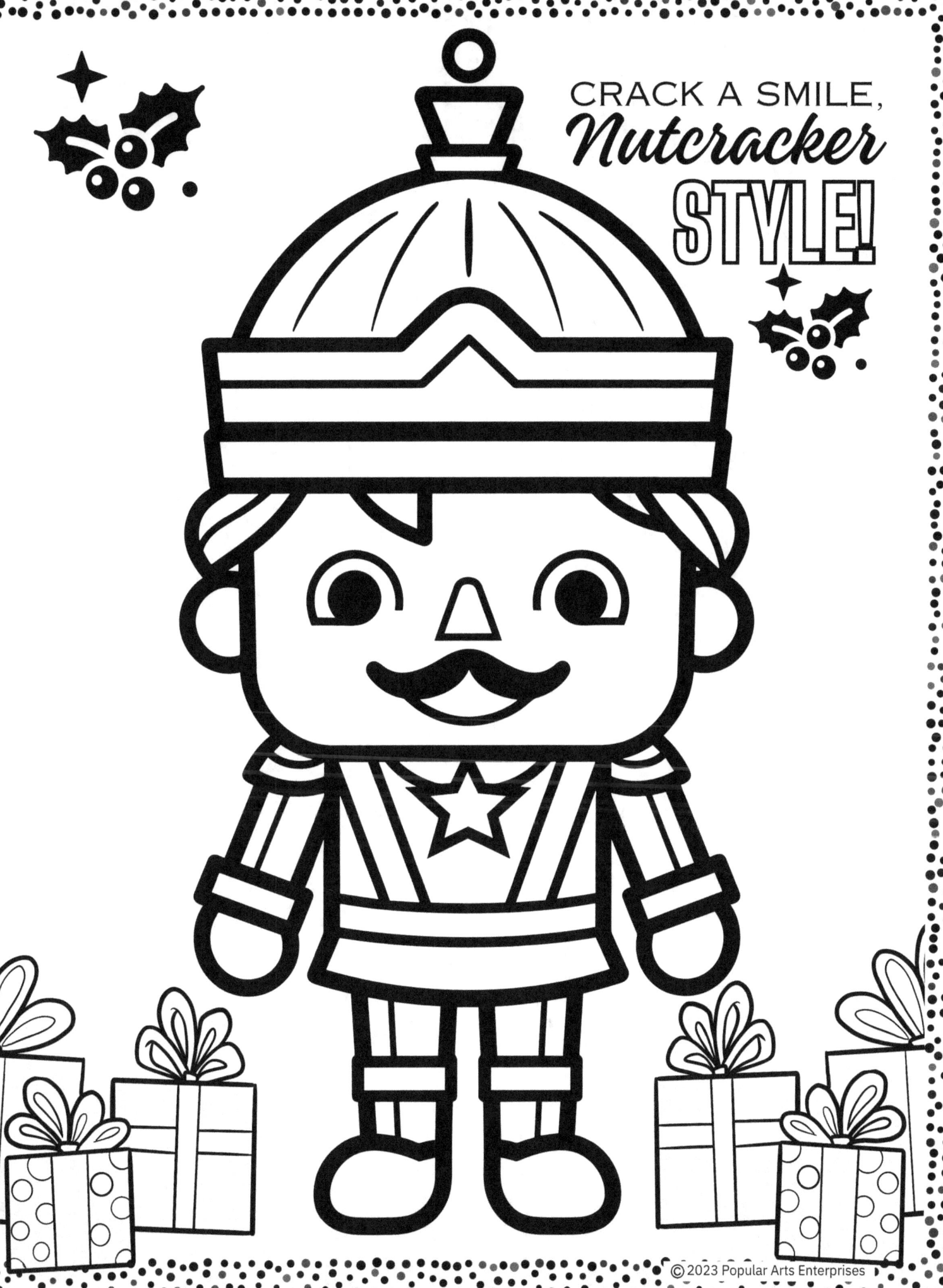

CRACK A SMILE,
Nutcracker
STYLE!

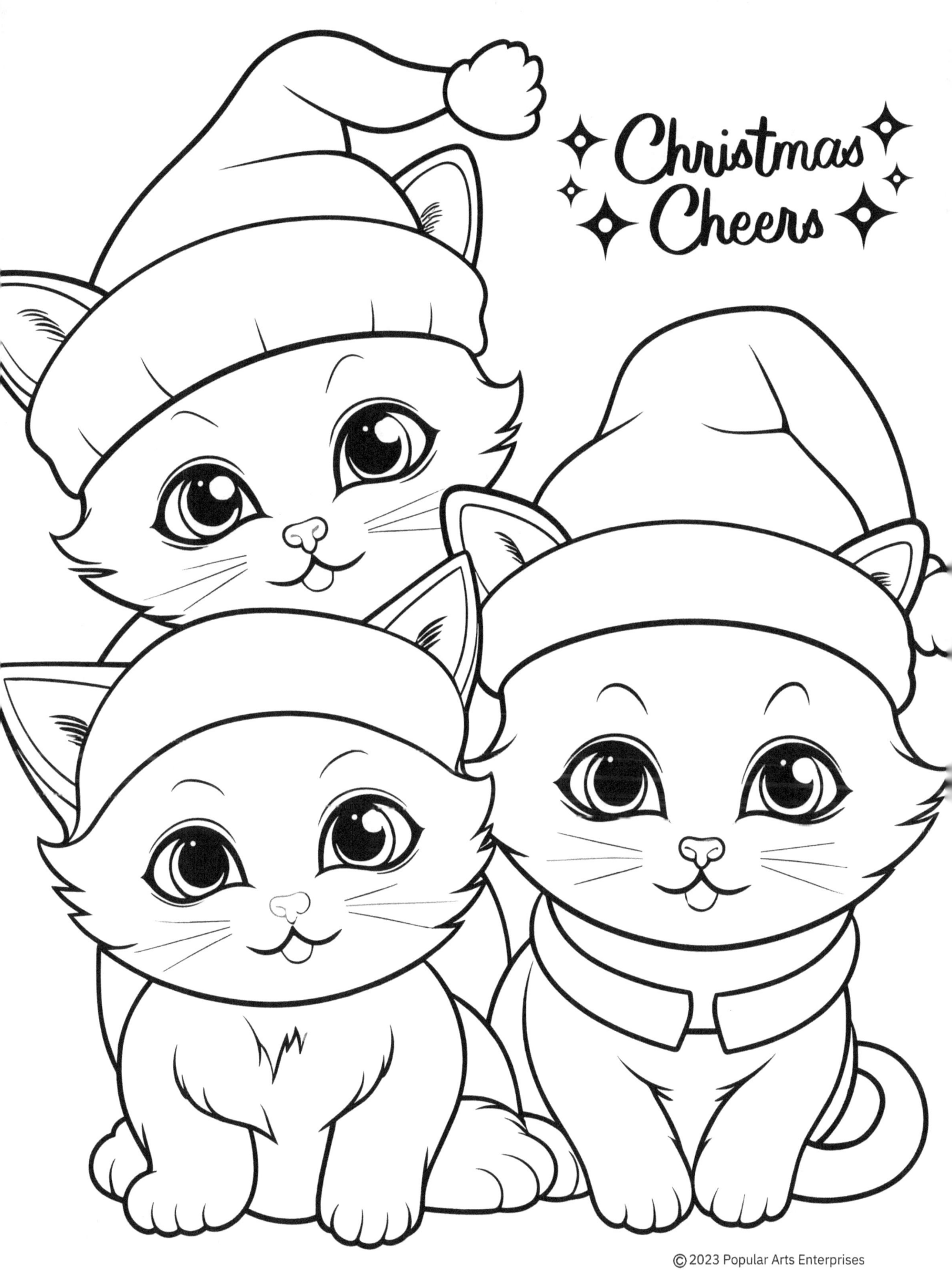

Christmas Cheers

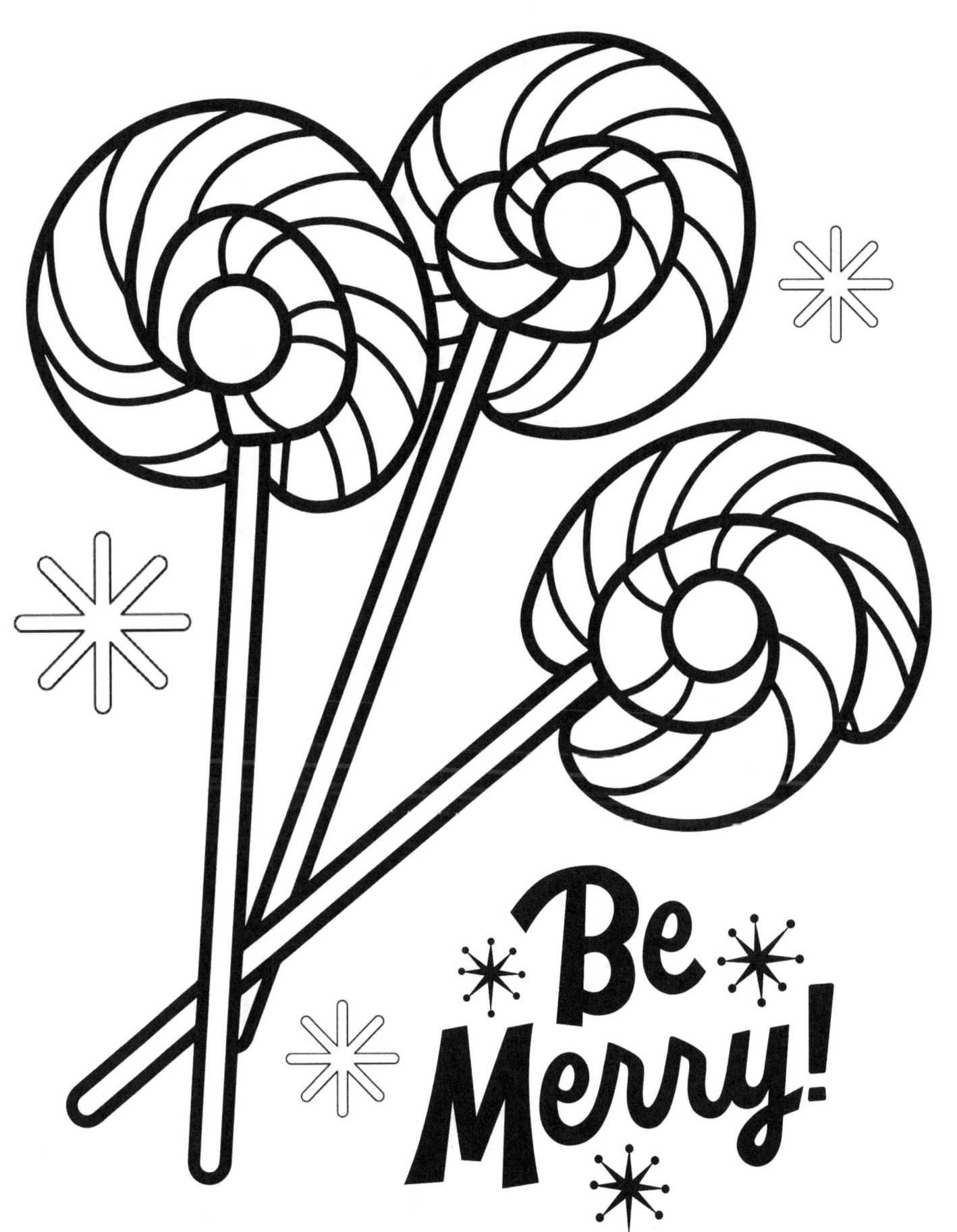

Be Merry!

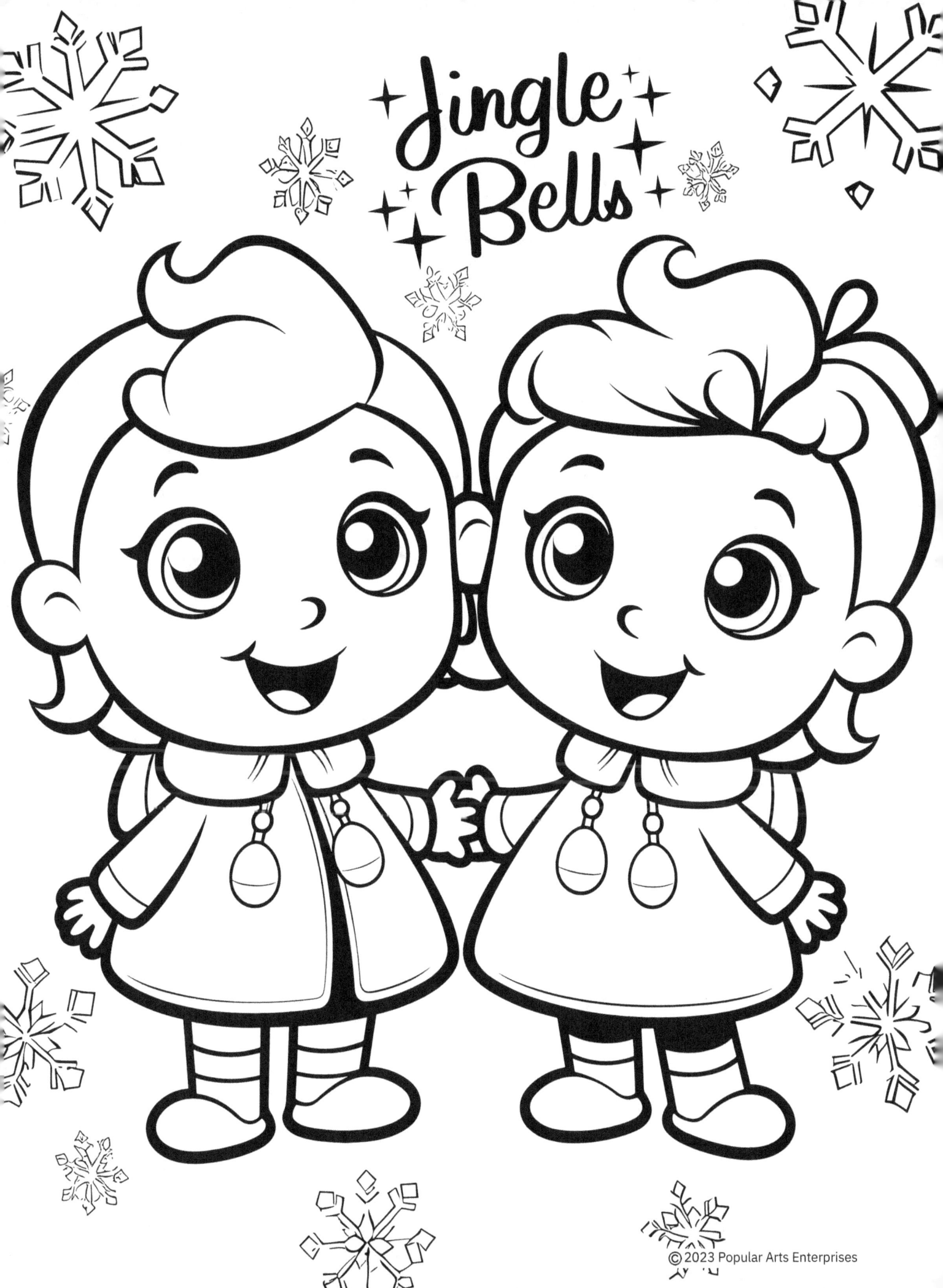

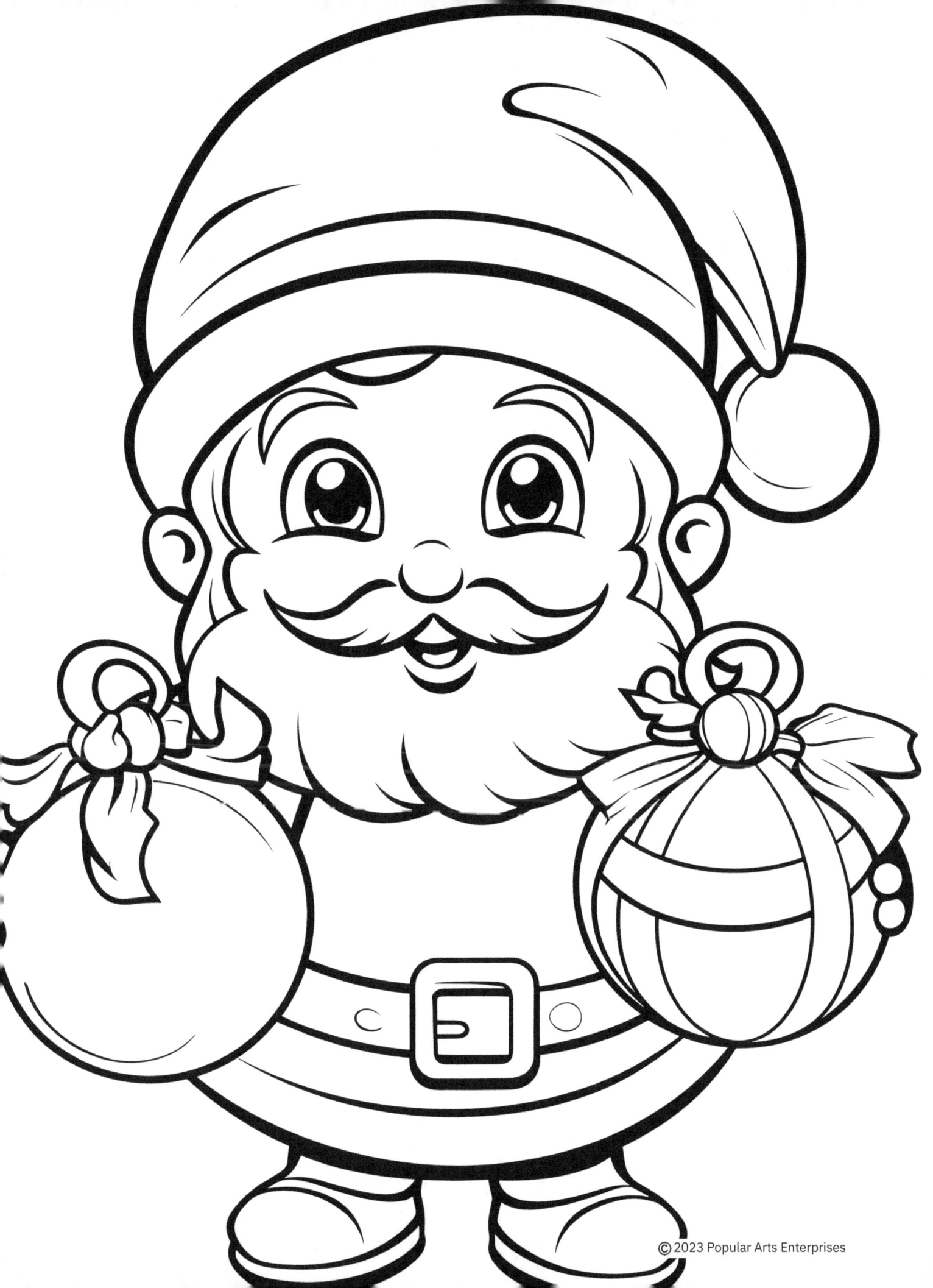

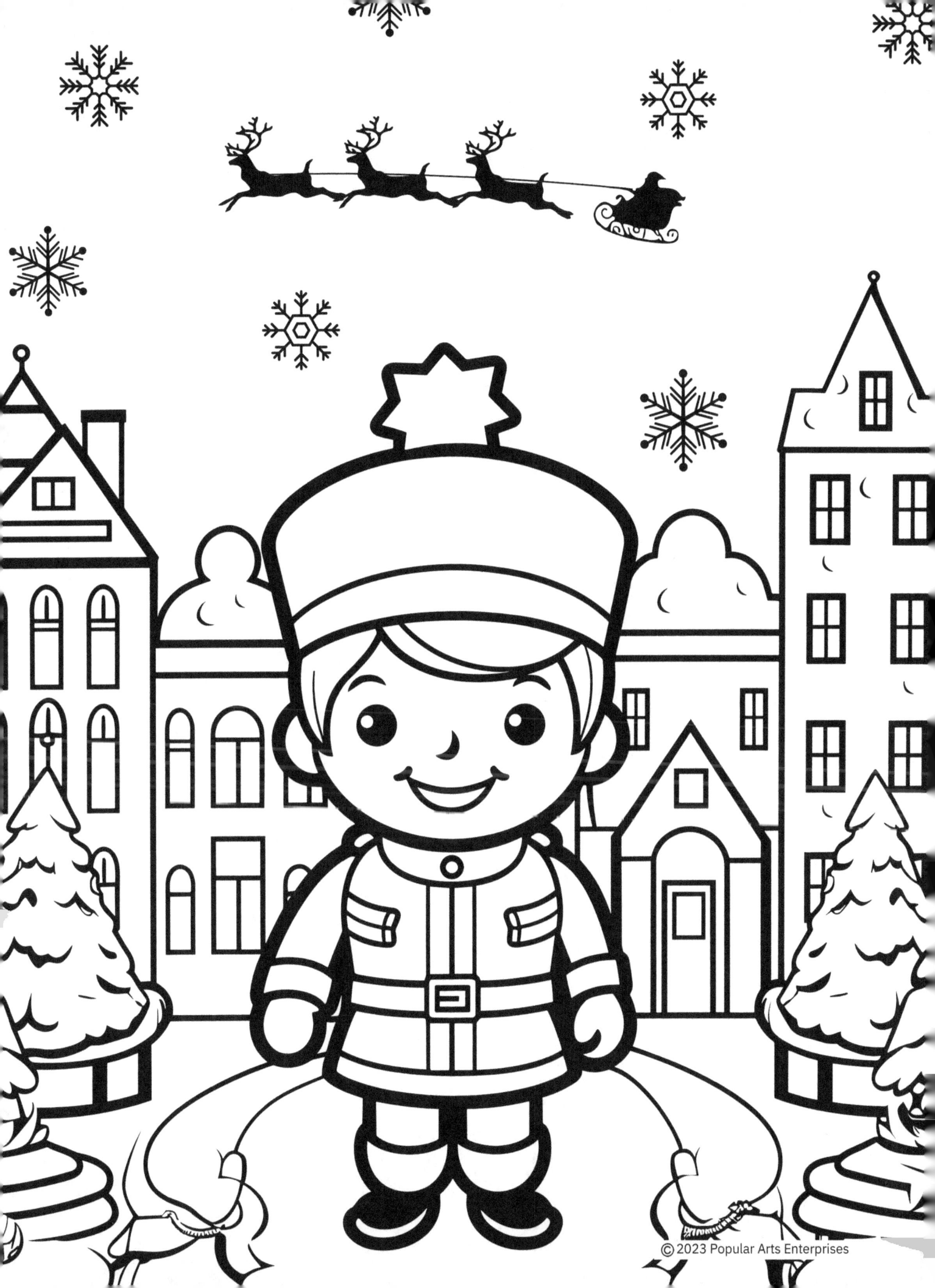

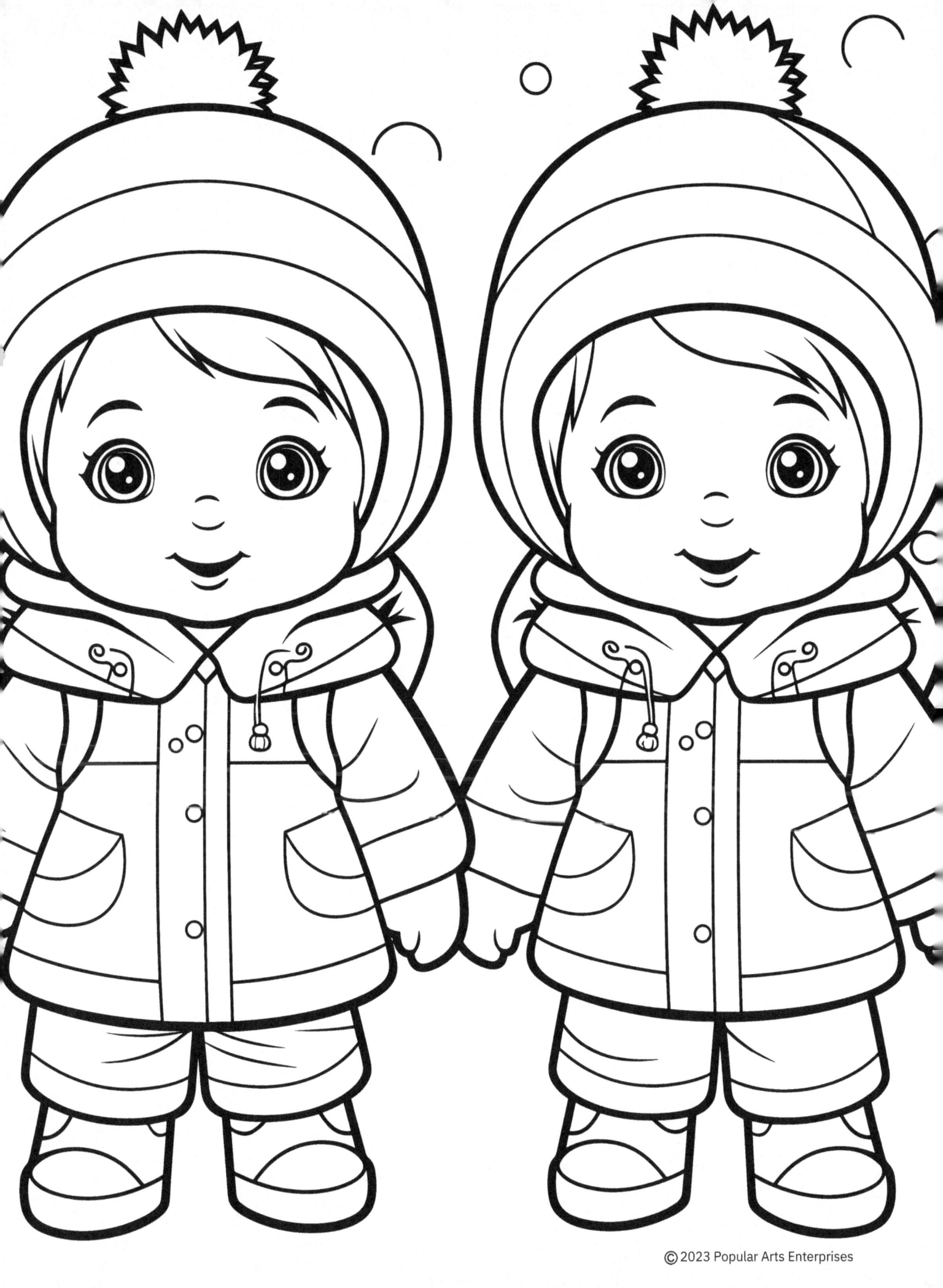

NUTS ABOUT Nutcracker!

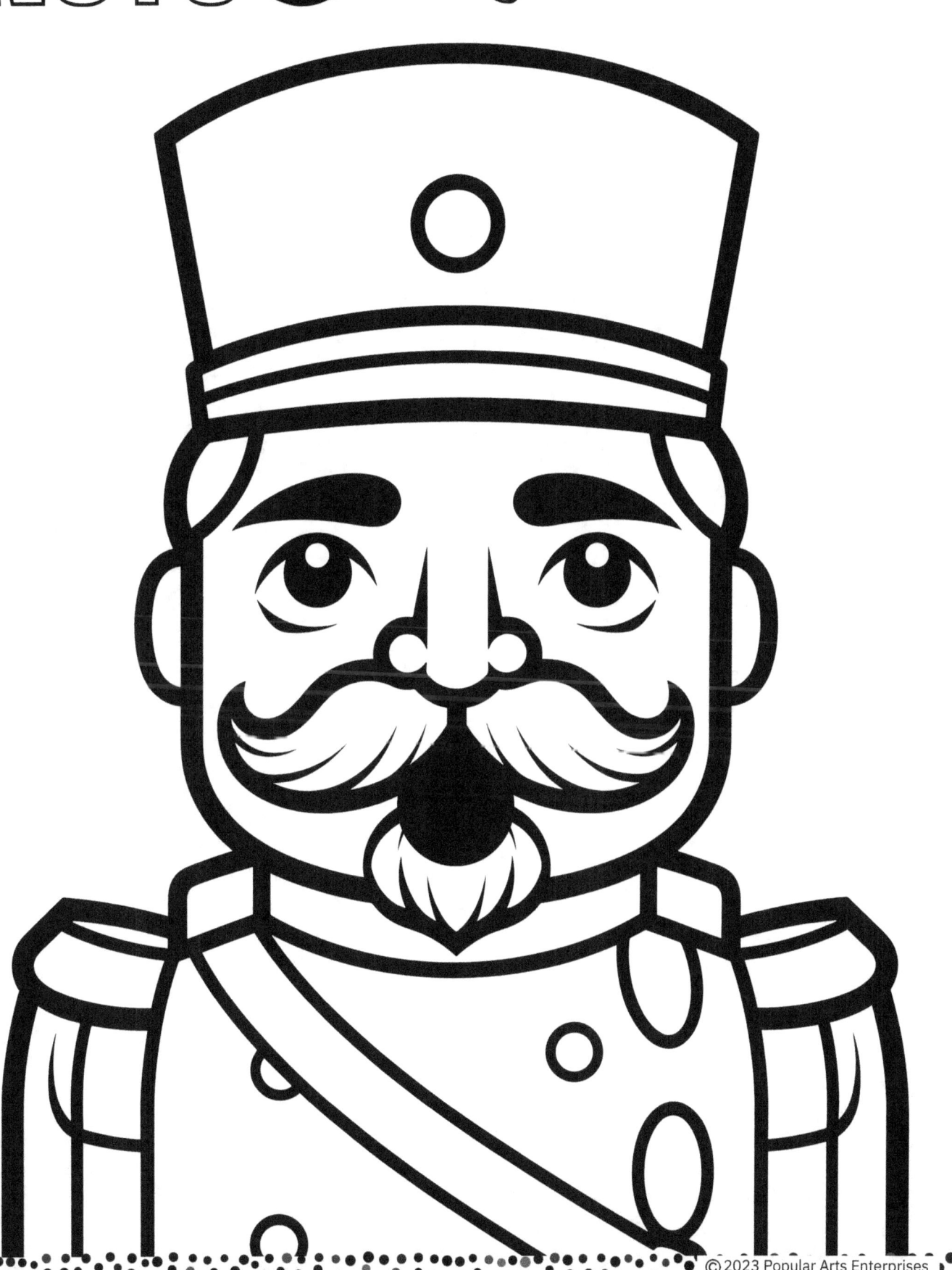

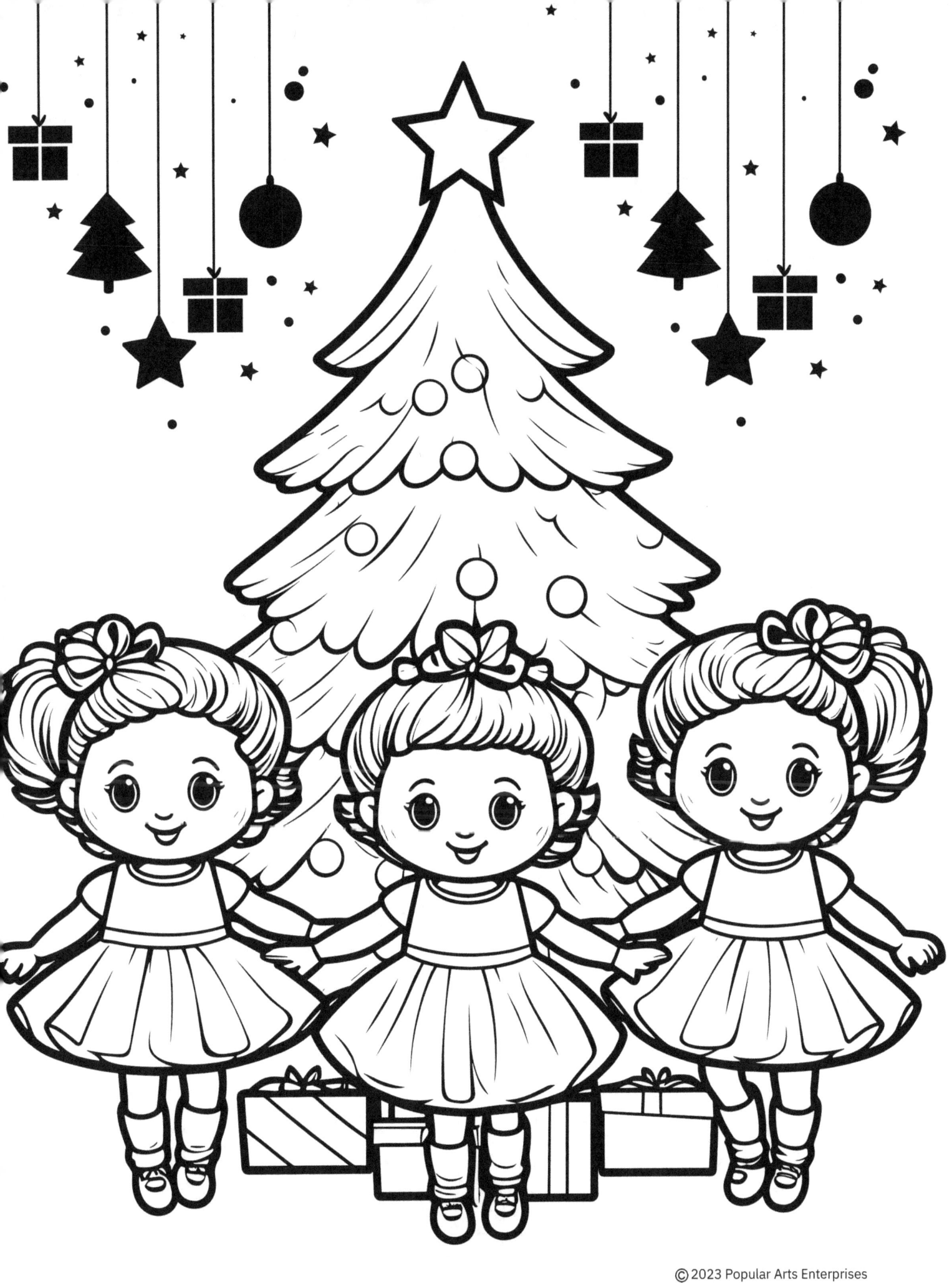

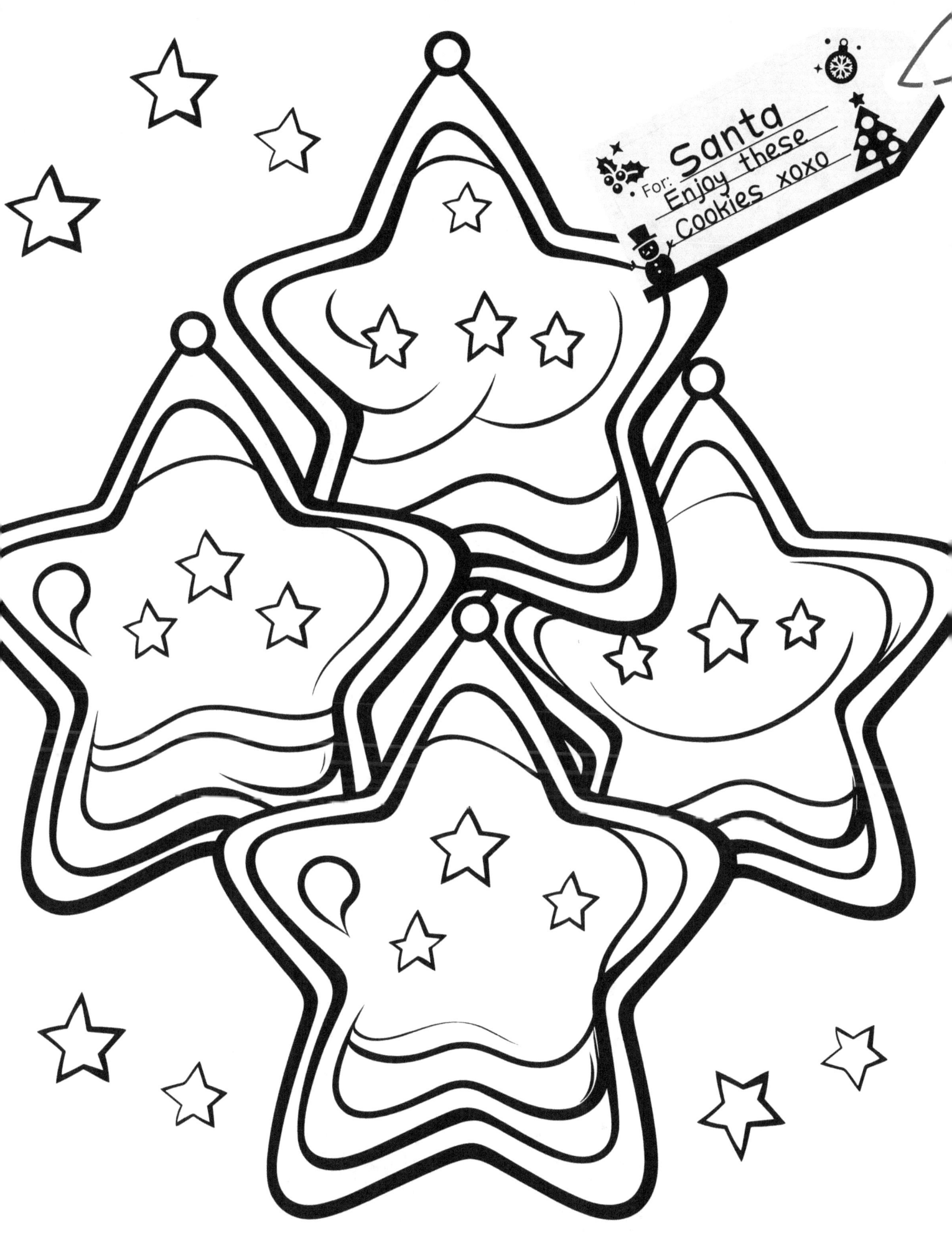

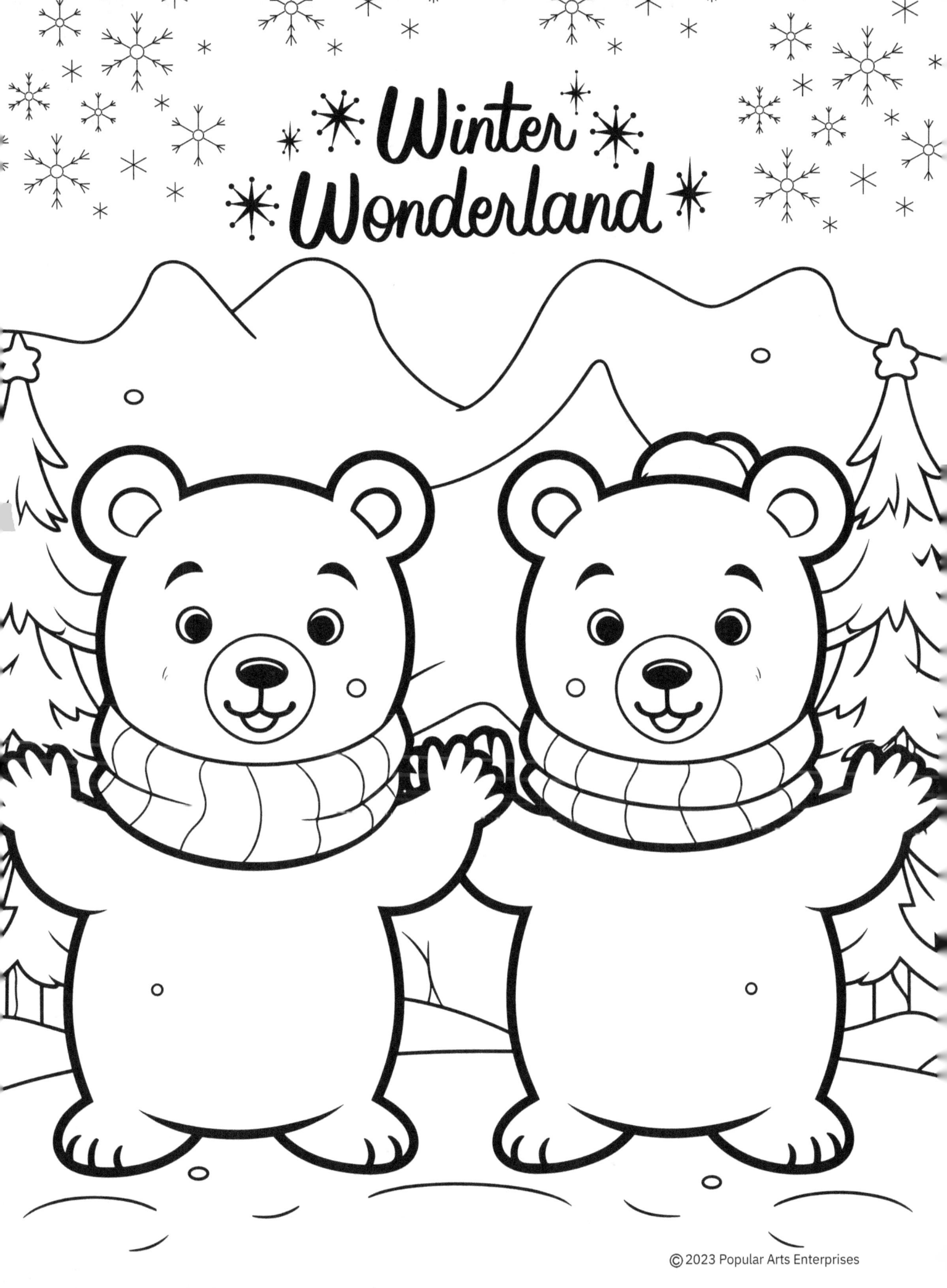

Happiness

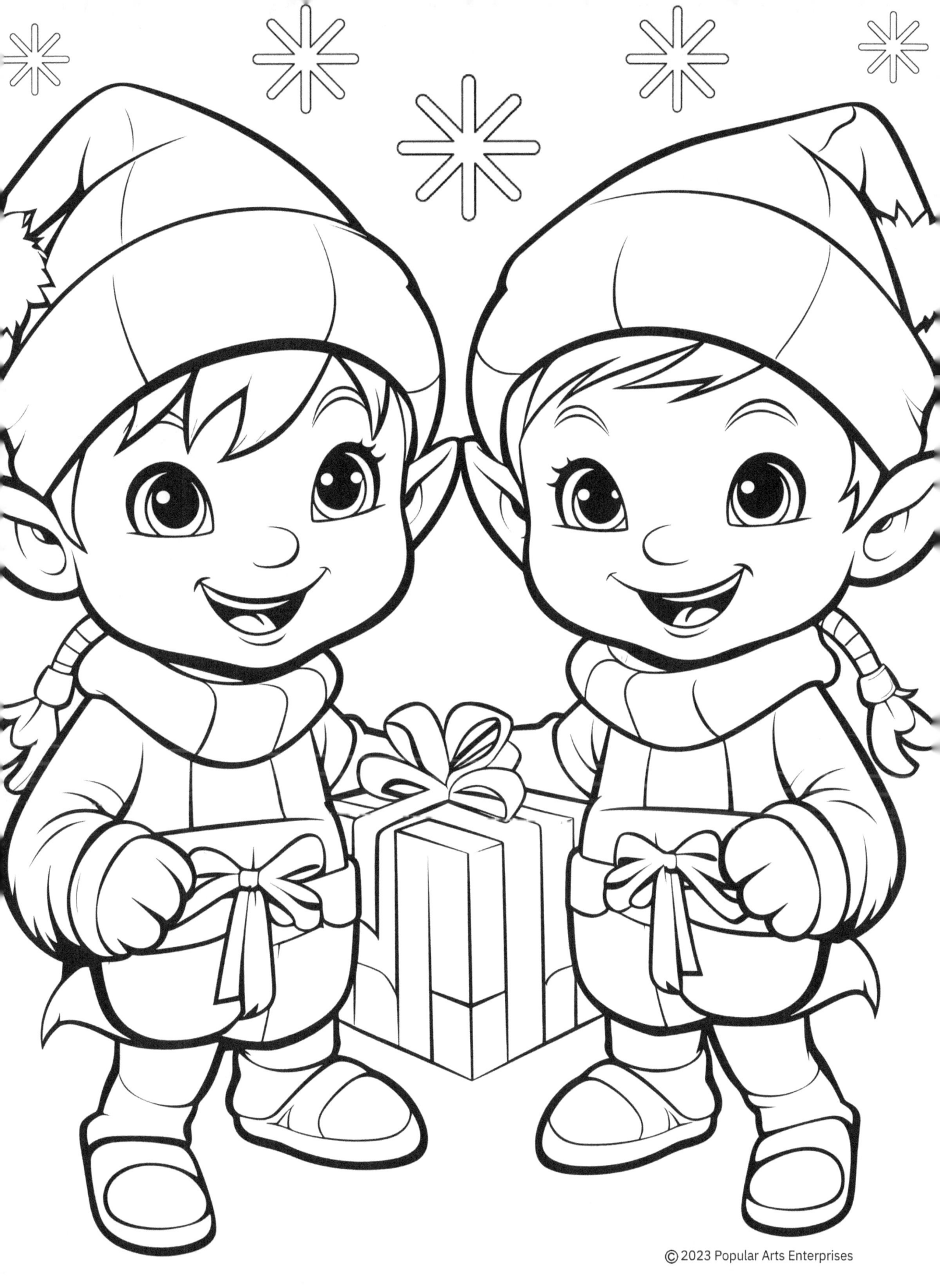

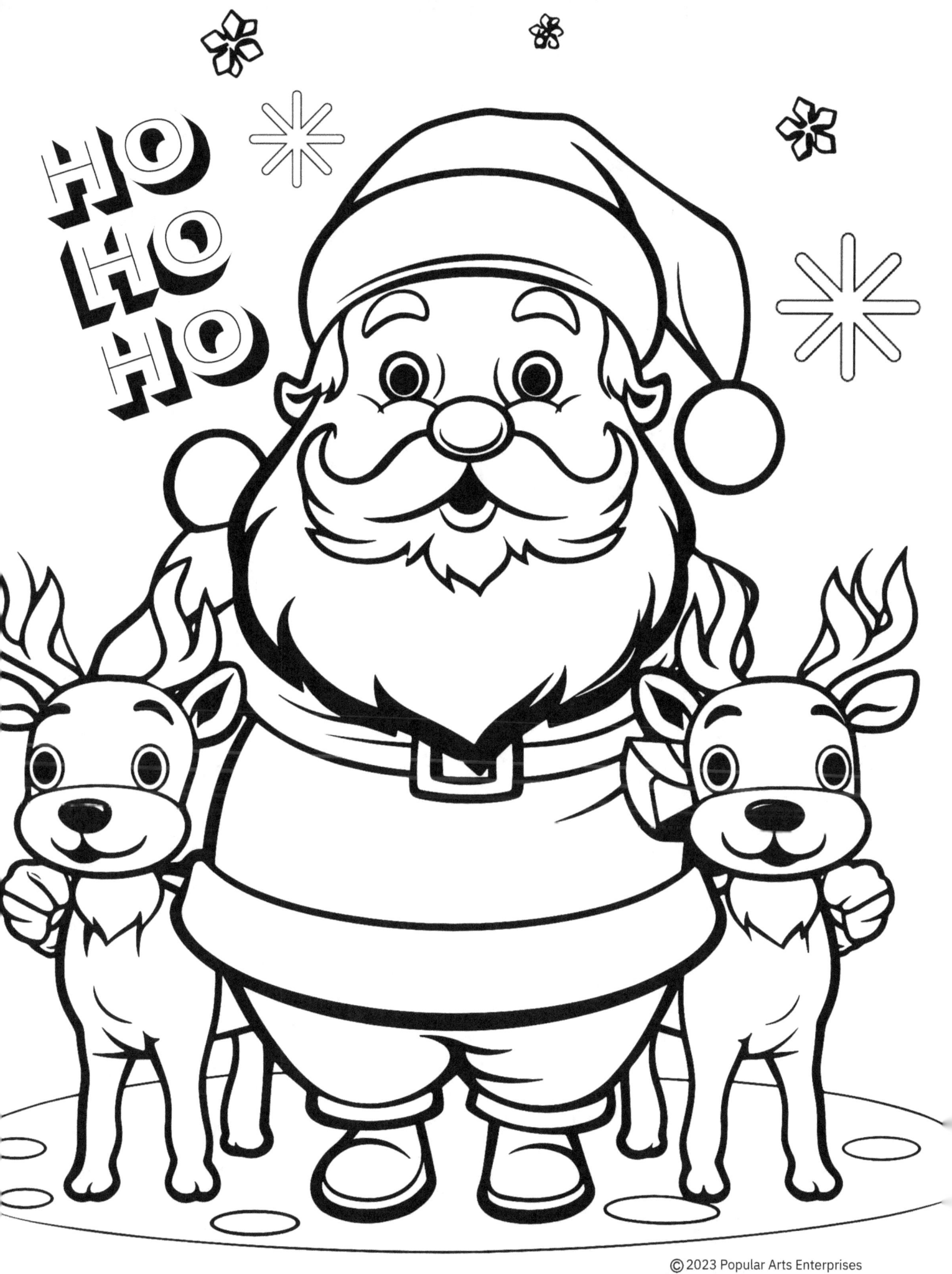

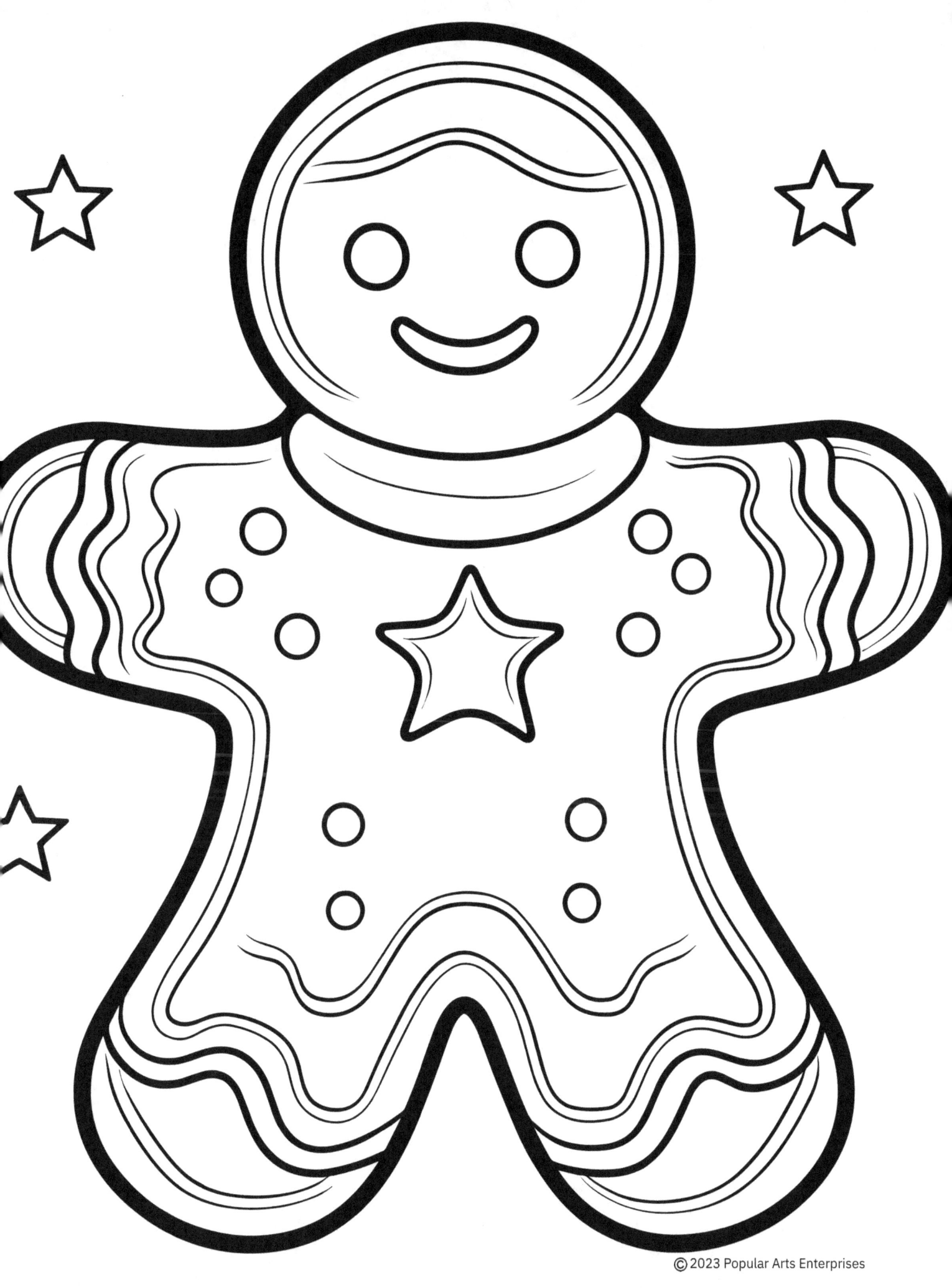

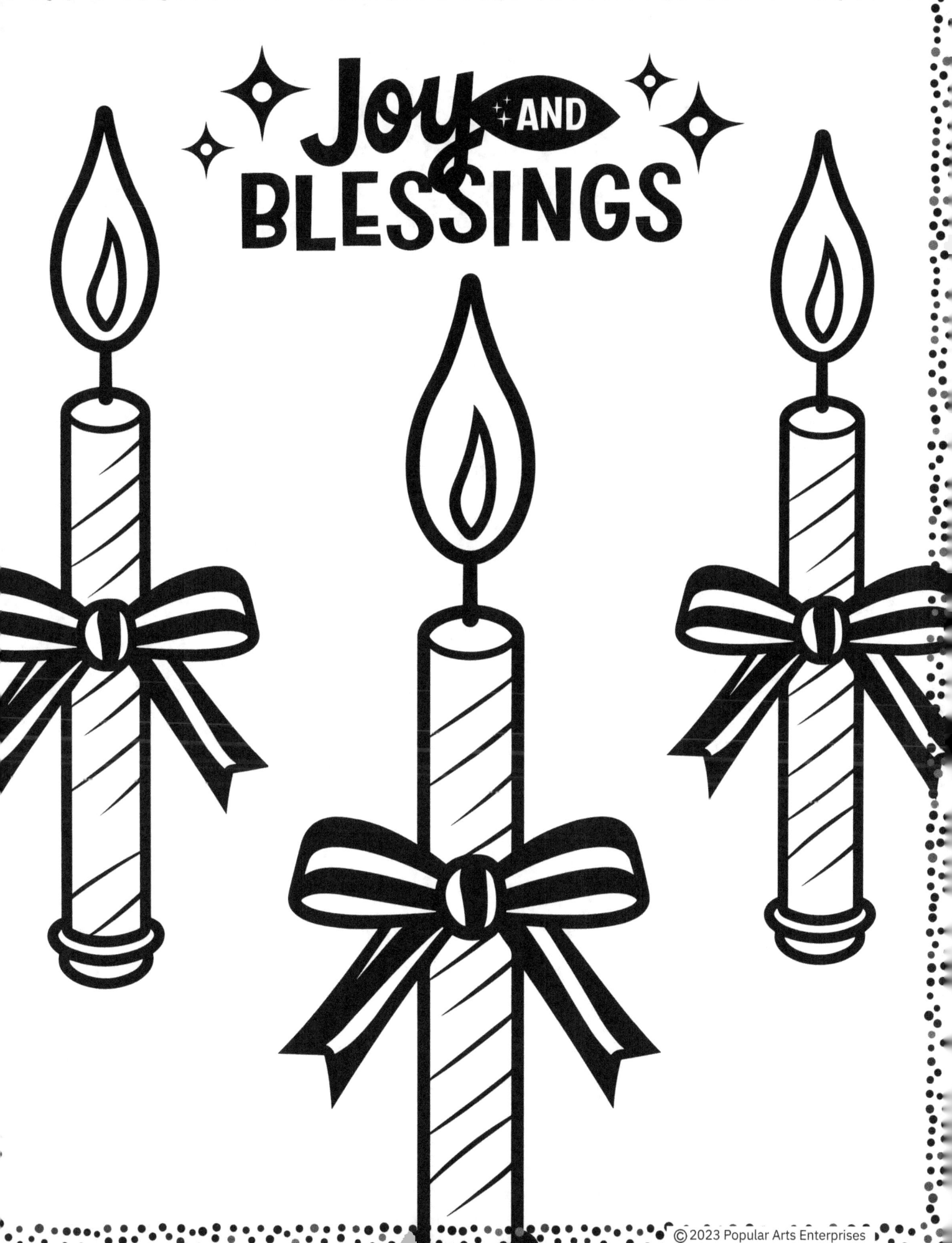

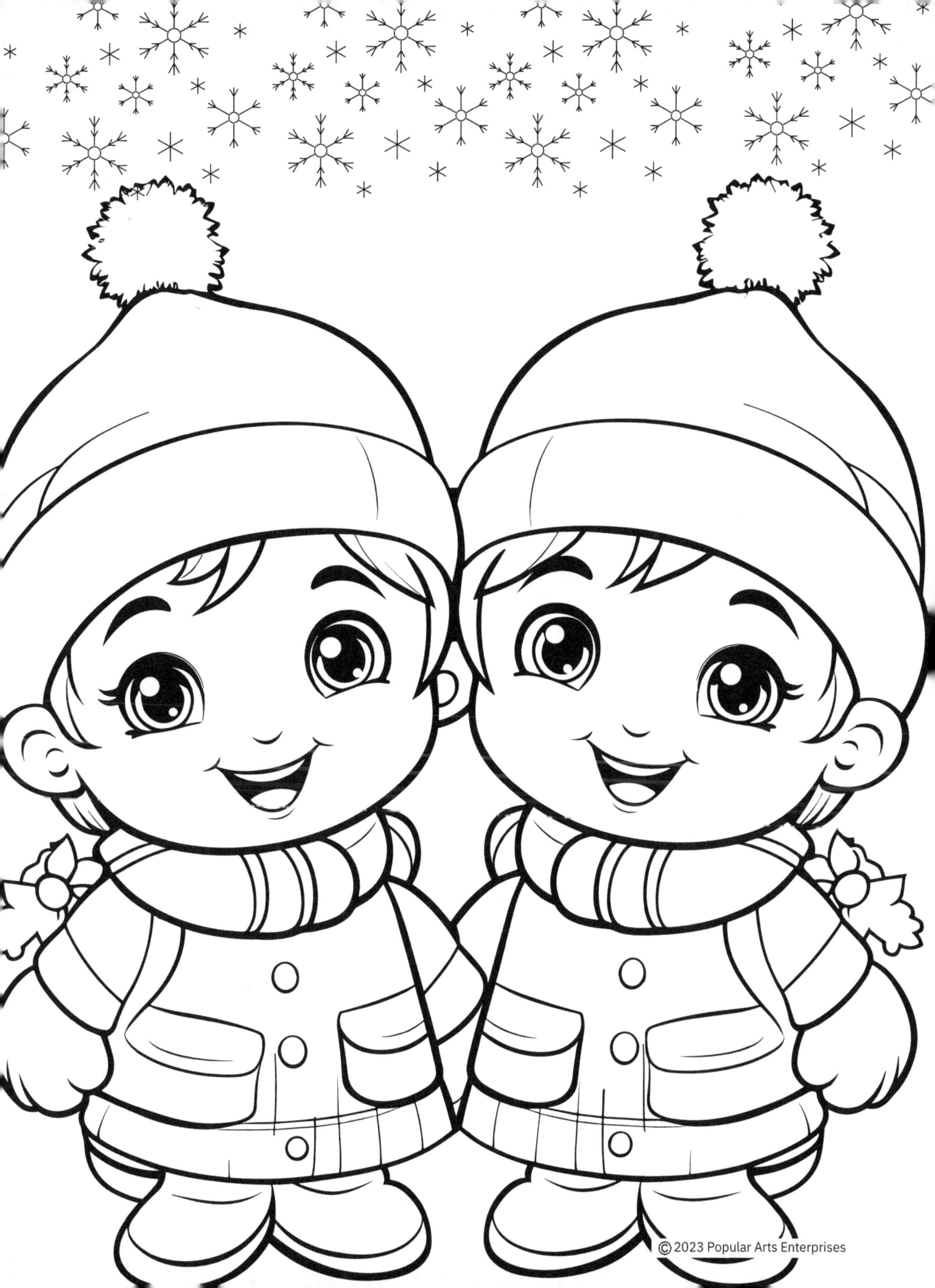

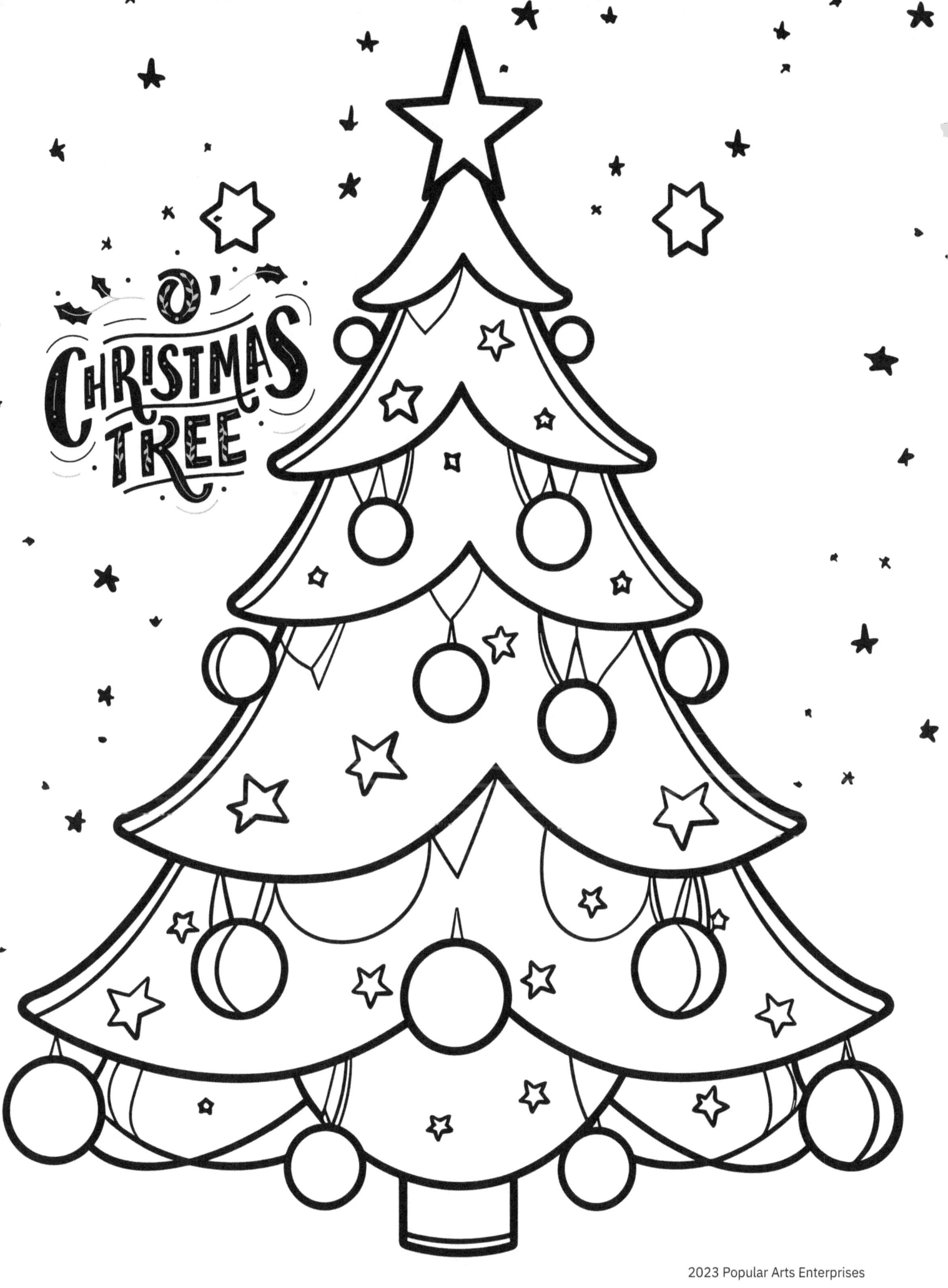

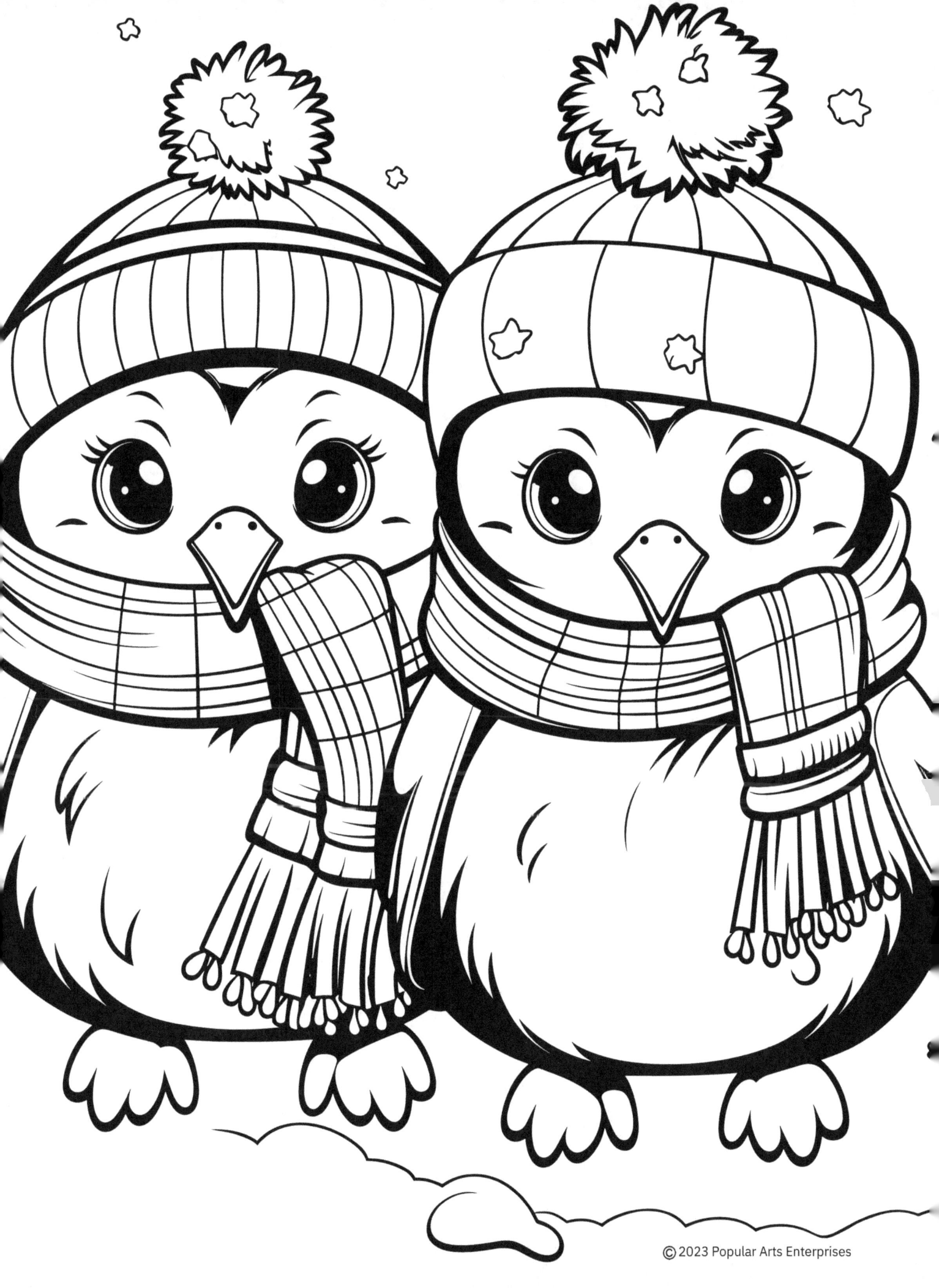

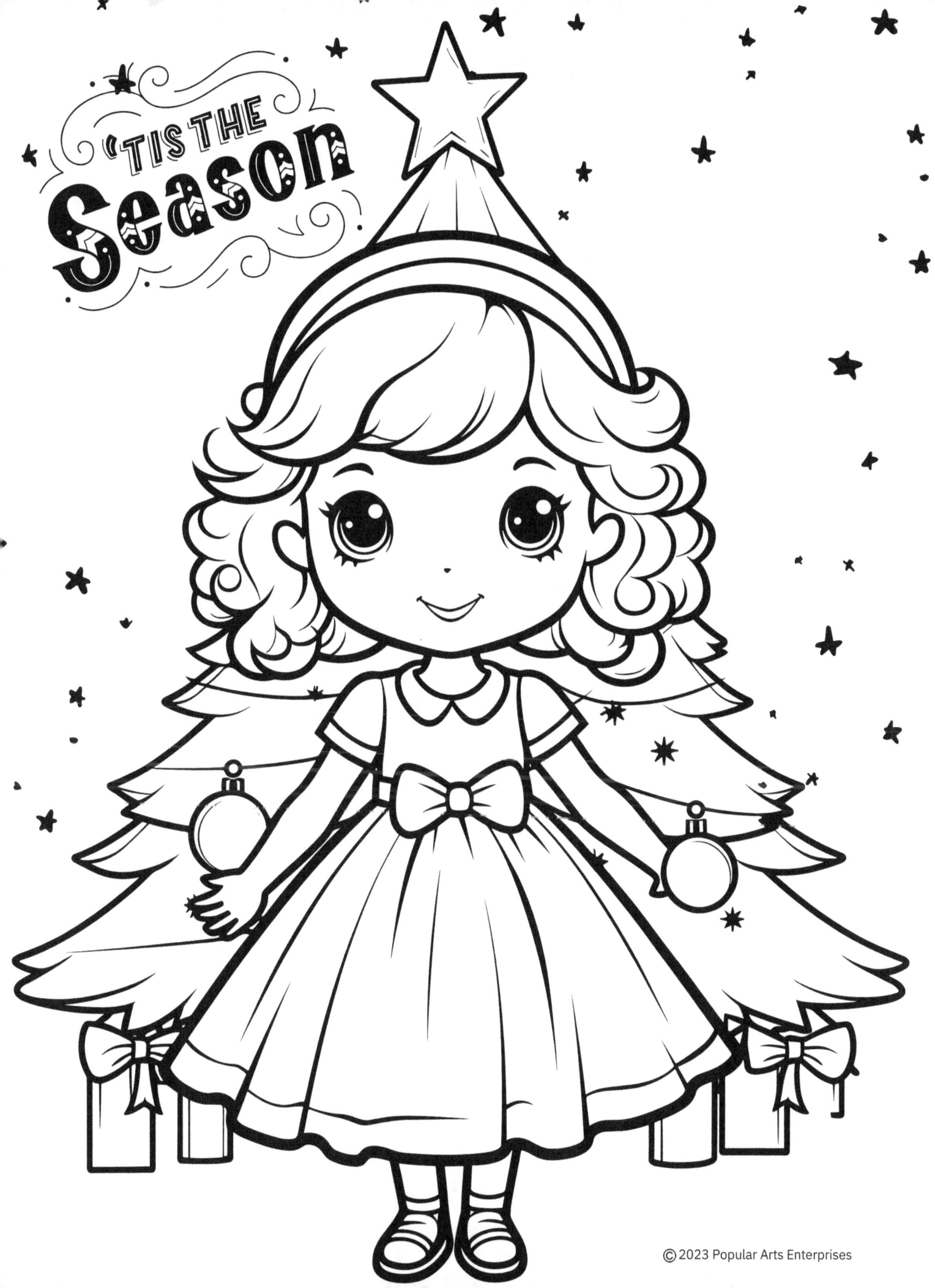

'TIS THE Season

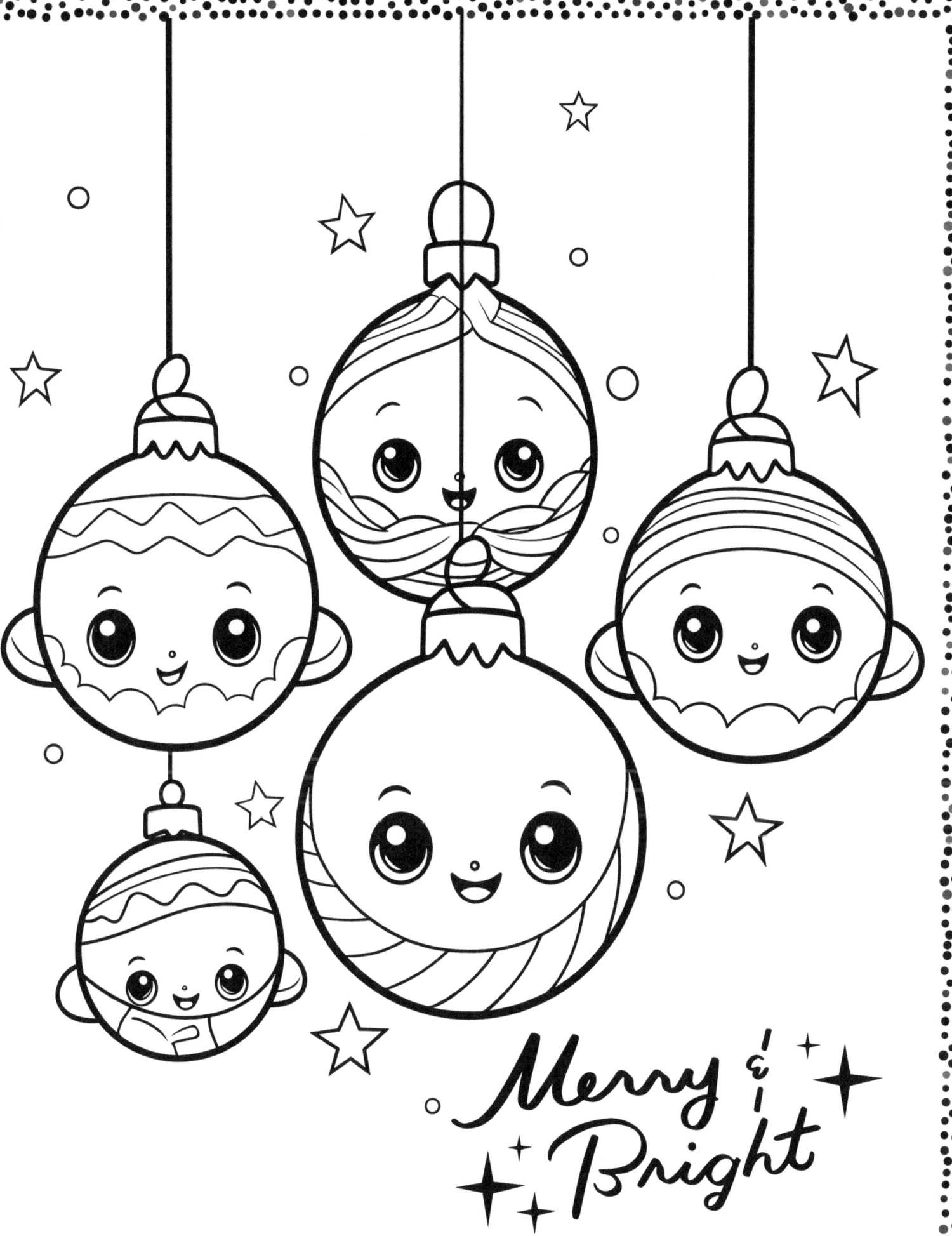

Merry & Bright

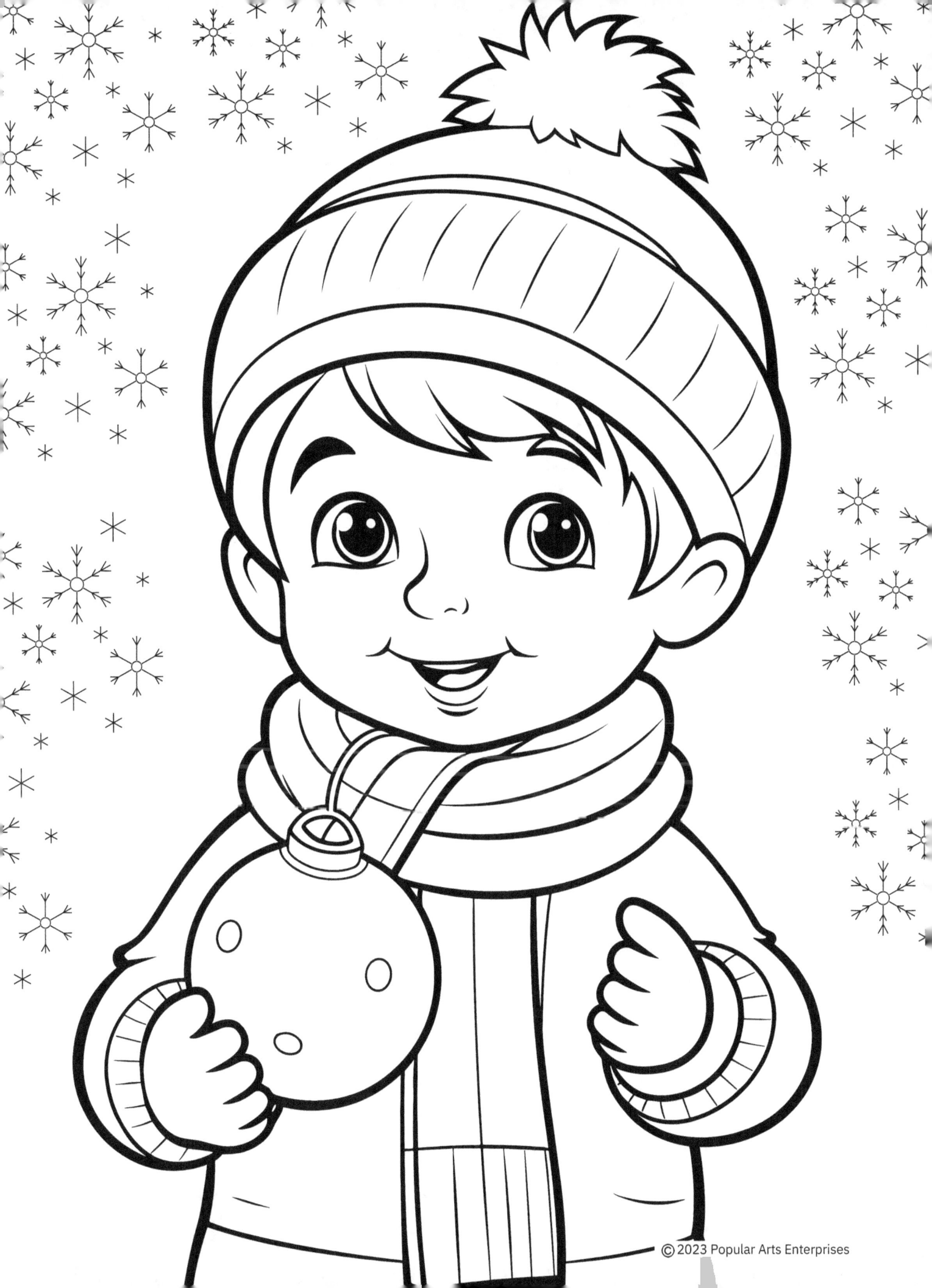

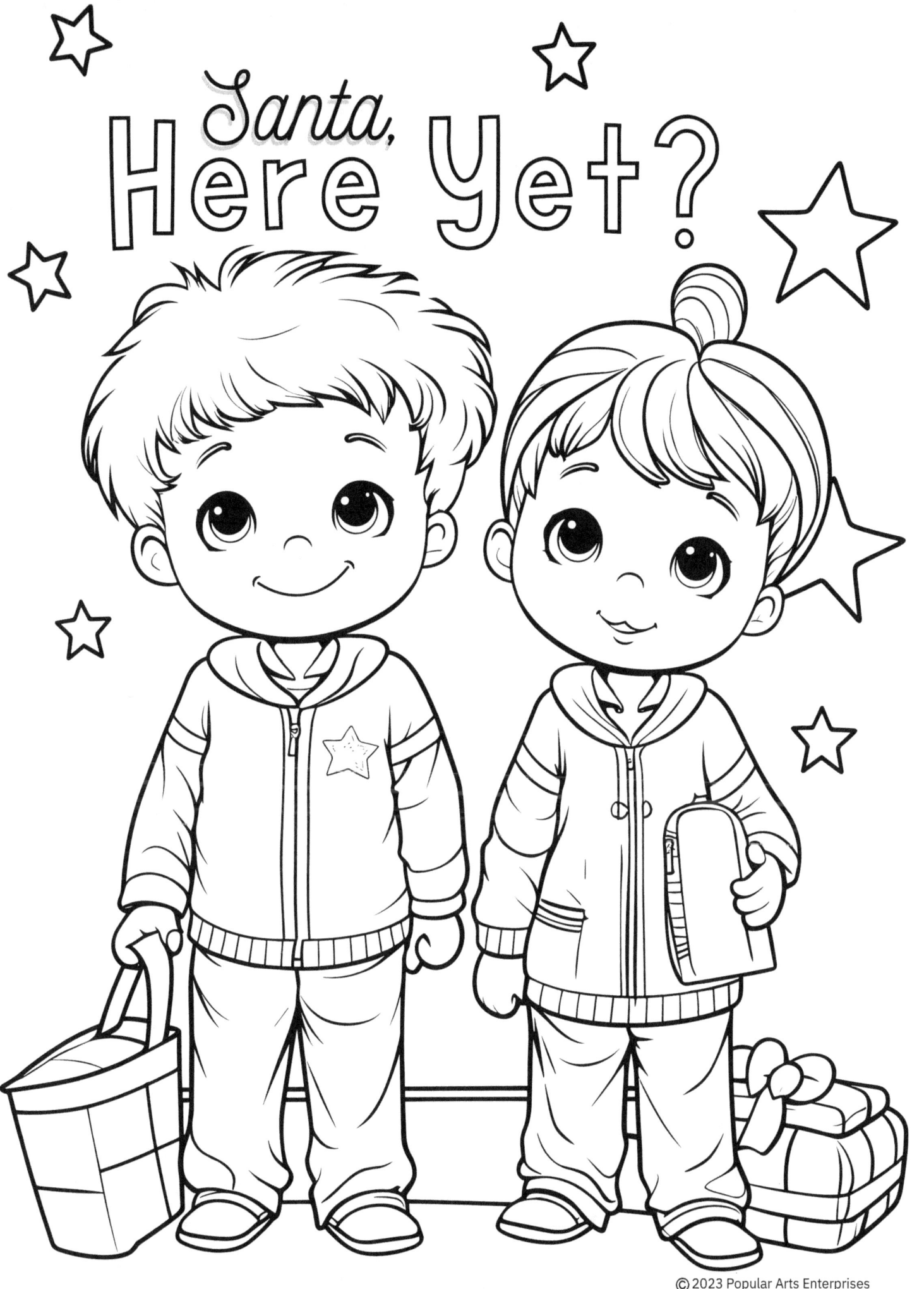

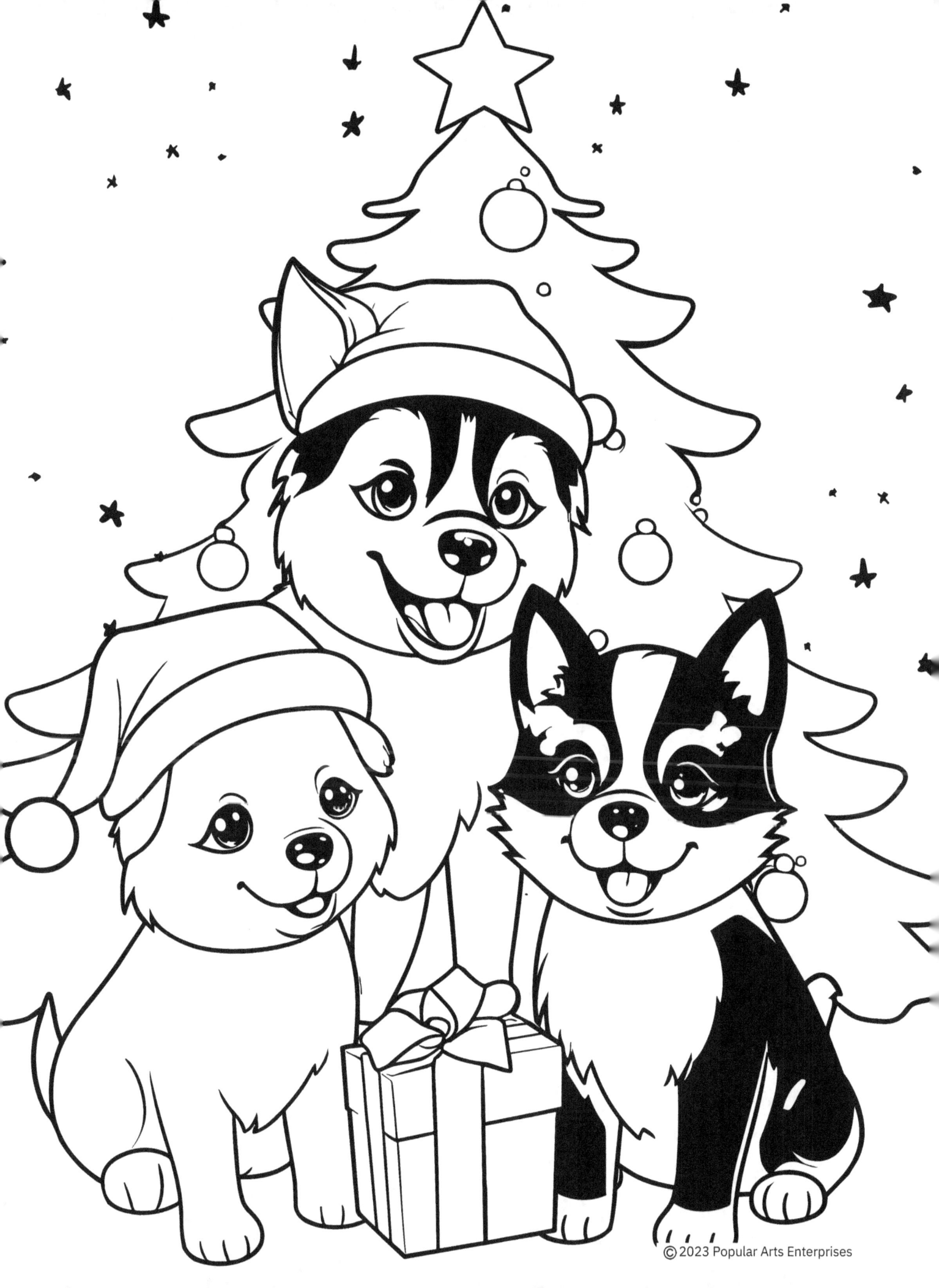

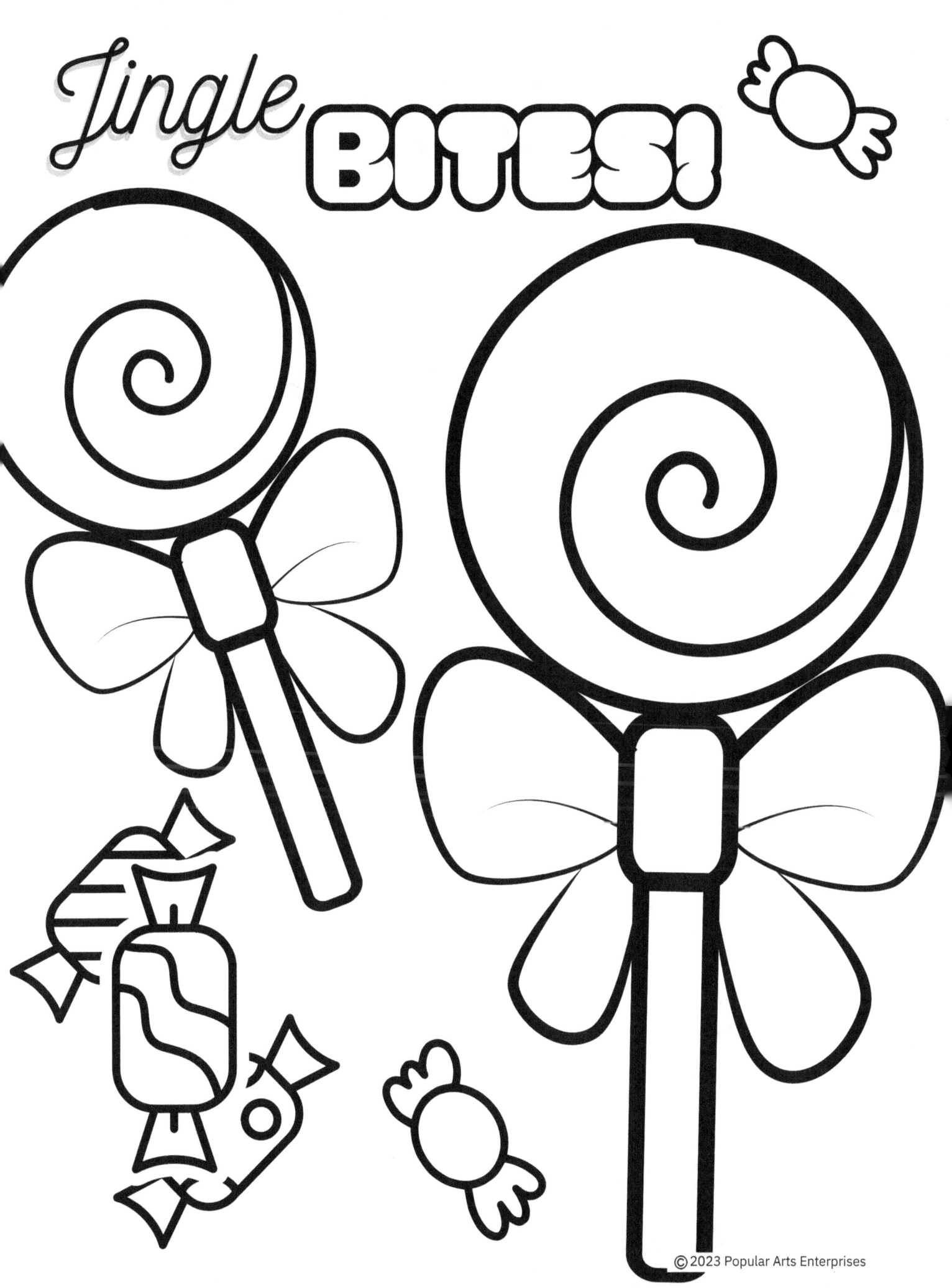

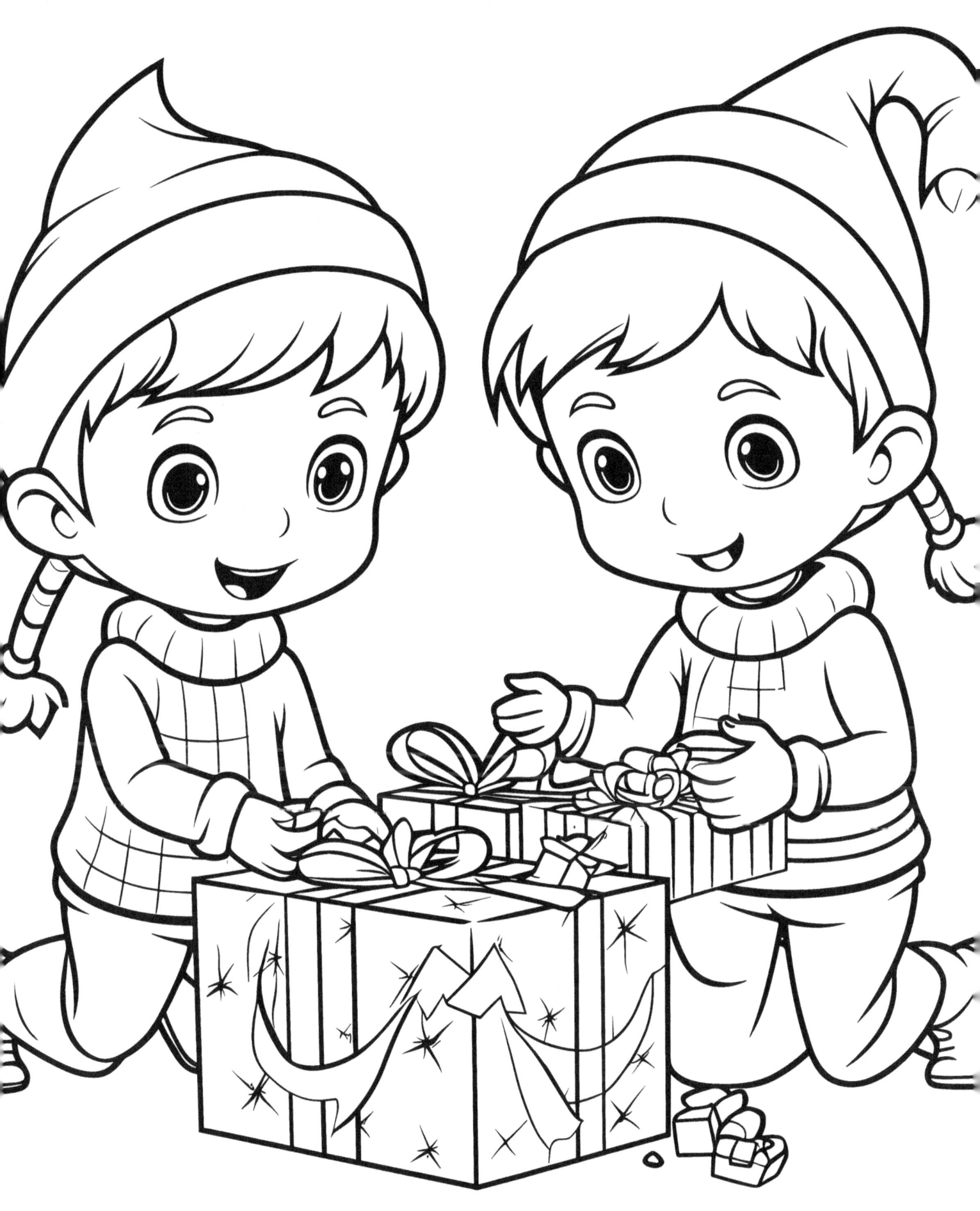

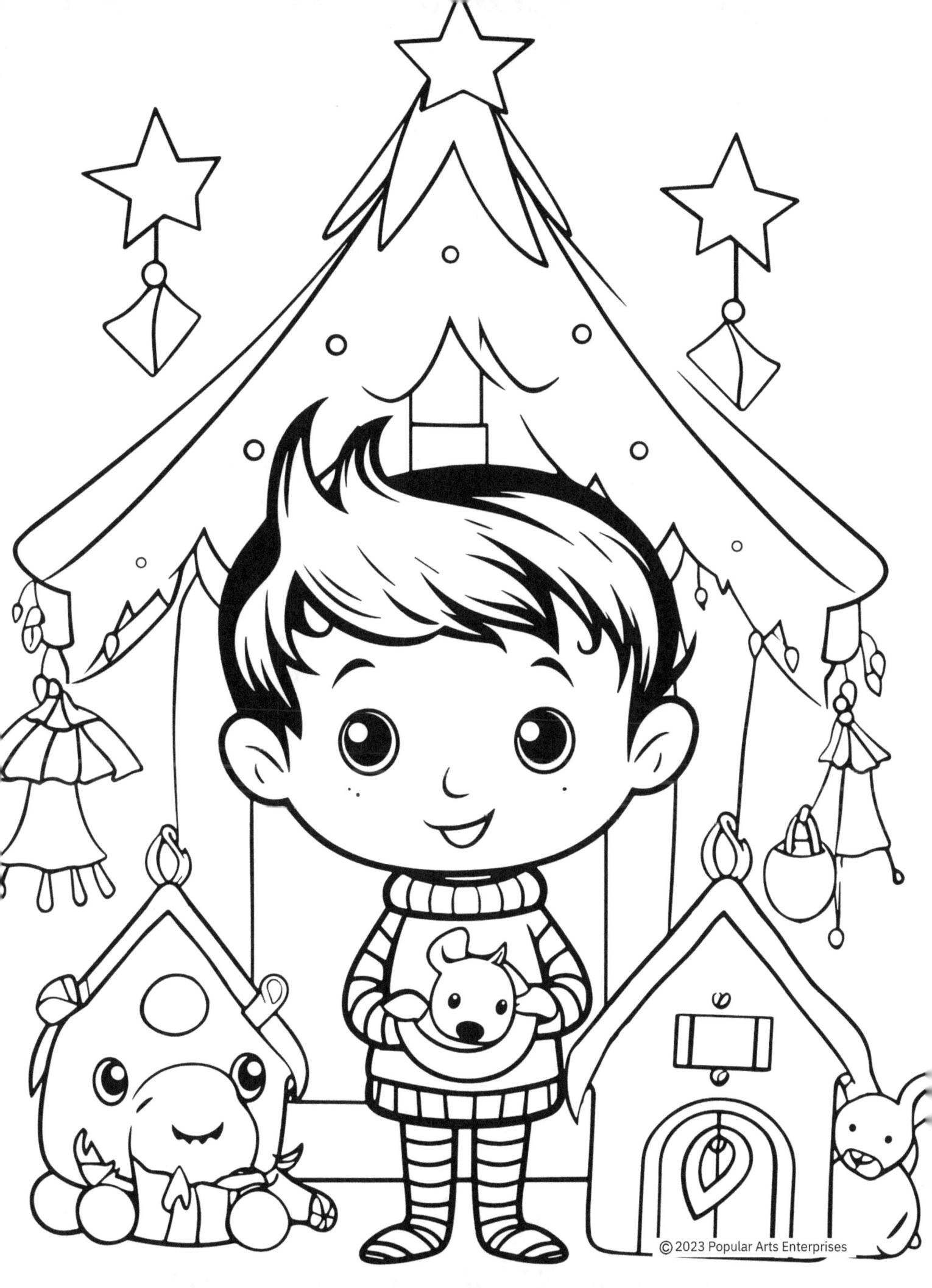

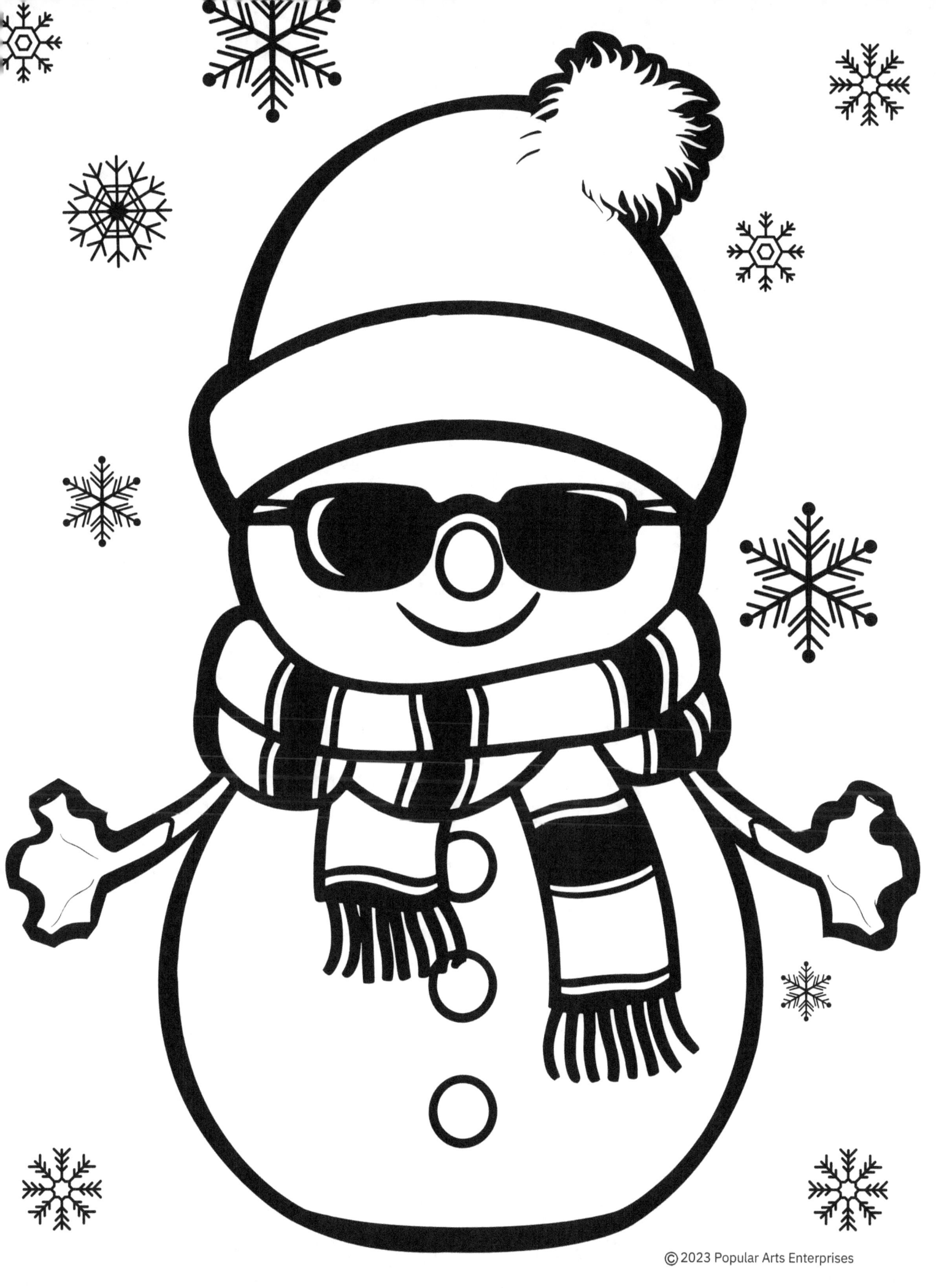

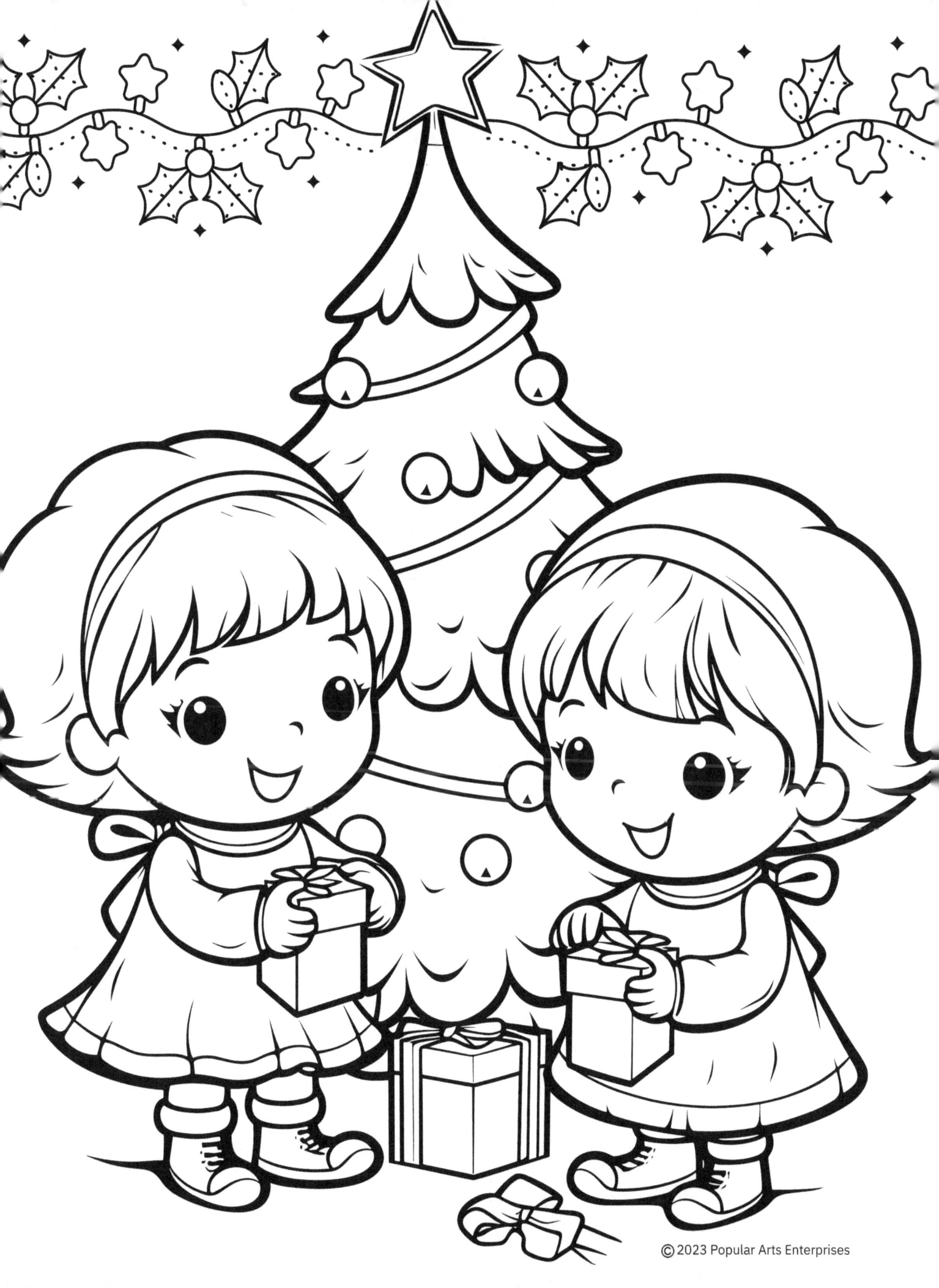

Thank You!

Don't be shy.... We want to hear from you!

We hope you enjoyed these fun and unique designs celebrating the spirit of Christmas.

Extra Bonus:

As our way of saying thanks we will email you, never before published, coloring pages. Takes 8 seconds! **(see below)**

Here's how to receive your FREE 8 coloring book pages:

1 Please scan the QR code. Leave a review on Amazon and feel free to attach a picture of your masterpiece.

+

=

2 Tag your artwork and follow us on social media (see below).
*Must have at least 10+ followers.

TikTok: @popularartspublishing

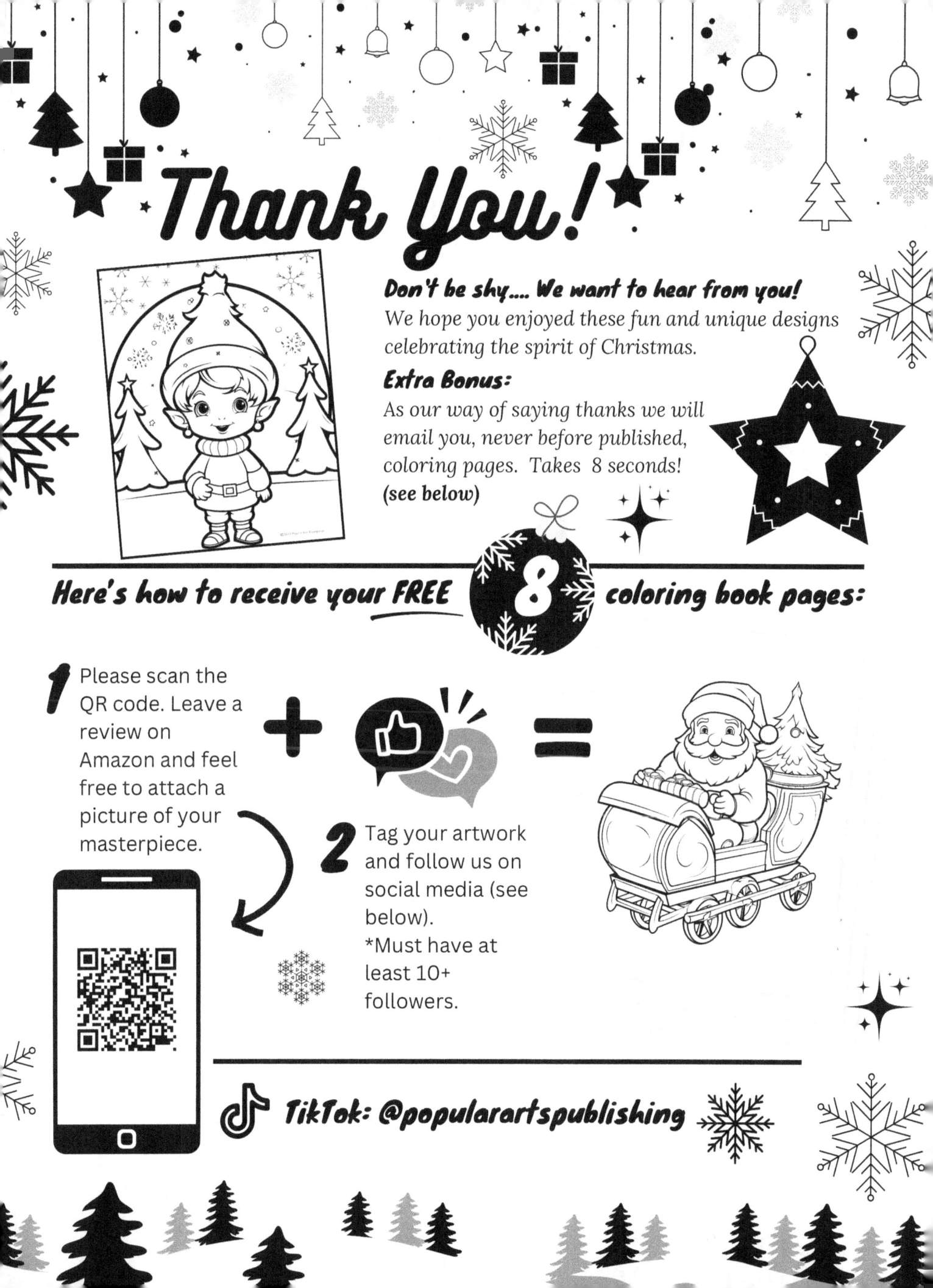